Shadow Games

The President's Gambit

BRADLEY KUHNS, PH.D., O.M.D.

Dedication

This work is dedicated to the brave investigators who delve into the darkest corners of power, where political wrongdoing and government corruption take root. Their tireless pursuit of truth, often in the face of immense pressure and personal risk, safeguards the very foundation of our society.

We honor their unwavering dedication to justice, meticulous attention to detail, and unwavering commitment to exposing the ugly truths others seek to conceal. They are the true guards of accountability, the heroes who stand up against the tide of deceit, ensuring that no individual is above the law, no matter how powerful.

These investigators' tireless efforts have brought down empires, toppled corrupt regimes, and held the highest officials accountable for their actions. They have shed light on hidden agendas, exposed webs of deceit, and given voice to the voiceless.

This dedication is not simply a recognition of their accomplishments but a testament to the courage they embody. It takes great strength to confront powerful interests, navigate intricate webs of misinformation, and persevere in adversity.

Their unwavering pursuit of justice inspires us all. It reminds us that even in the darkest times, the flame of truth can burn brightly, fueled by the courage and dedication of those who dare to seek it.

May their legacy inspire future generations of investigators, journalists, and whistleblowers to fight for transparency, accountability, and a free and just society.

With deepest respect and admiration,

(Bradley W. Kuhns, Former Investigator)

About the Author

Bradley Kuhns transitioned through three exciting careers during his life. The first was as a Las Vegas performer and musician.

His second career was in law enforcement which allowed him to work within the elite ranks of the Los Angeles Police Department (LAPD), Scientific Investigation Division. He utilized his acquired skills of investigation, interrogation, polygraph (lie detection), and forensic hypnosis to assist not only the LAPD, but other city, county, state, and federal agencies as well, to solve some of the most heinous crimes perpetrated in America.

Bradley's third career, after earning a clinical psychology degree and a Doctor of Oriental Medicine degree maintained a private practice in Marriage and Family therapy.

Author's Note

This gripping tale of crime, suspense, and intrigue you hold in your hands is purely a work of fiction. While the events and characters may seem eerily real, they are the product of the author's imagination and do not reflect actual individuals, businesses, or incidents. Any resemblance to real-world persons, living or dead, is purely coincidental.

Slip into a fictional tale, where every word is spun from the author's mind. No real-life counterpart exists for people and places you'll encounter, allowing you to lose yourself in the story.

Immerse yourself in a universe crafted solely for your enjoyment. Your experiences and events are purely brushstrokes, designed to transport you far from the boundaries of reality.

Though the world within may feel somewhat familiar, rest assured the individuals and events are entirely fictional. While the themes explored might resonate with real-world issues, the individuals at the heart of this story are purely fictional creations. No specific person or organization is intended to be represented.

It's all just make-believe.

Happy reading.

Preface

For years, I have walked the tightrope between mundane paperwork and the macabre reality of the criminal world. As an investigator working in the trenches of law enforcement, I have witnessed humanity in its darkest corners, where lives were shattered and the line between good and evil blurred beyond recognition.

My journey took me through the twisting corridors of municipal, county, state, and federal investigations. No crime was too small, no evil too vast, from petty thefts, the cold-blooded killer, and the white-collar wolf in sheep's clothing to heinous atrocities. I saw it all unfold alongside dedicated investigators, each with their own scars etched by the cases they carried.

However, amidst the darkness, a silver light remained: the pursuit of justice. Witnessing criminals face the consequences of their actions, standing before a jury of their peers, and finally being held accountable for the lives that they had marred brought a sense of bittersweet satisfaction.

This book is a testament to those unseen battles, a chronicle of the countless faces etched in my memory – the victims, the perpetrators, and the silent witnesses to a world teetering on the edge. It is a glimpse into the dark corners where justice fights to be served, a tale woven from the threads of experience, where the line of right and wrong blurs in the hushed silence of the corridors of power.

Be warned, the stories you are about to embark on will challenge your perception of reality and leave you questioning the depths of human depravity. But remember, even in the coldest corners, a spark for justice can still ignite.

Turn the page and enter a world, where darkness holds sway, but a sliver of hope still exists.

Prepare to be consumed.

Contents

Chapter One:
The Viper In The Nest

The dull buzz of the lights amplified the tension crackling in the air. Lt. General Adams paced the secure room somewhere, in the Pentagon, his face carved with worry lines—a history of battles fought and burdens carried. Years left their impression on him, his hair graying underneath the sharp folds of his cap.

Storm-clouded eyes beneath a furrowed brow mirrored the hurricane raging inside and flickered towards the reinforced door every few seconds, a restless energy coursing through his battle-hardened physique.

A short beard flecked with silver framed a jaw clenched tight, battling concealed concerns. Even the crisp uniform struggled to contain his broad shoulders, still soldier-straight, each crease a whisper of campaigns past. A weathered giant, rigid and strong, every line in his face was a story of service and sacrifice.

The door creaked open, admitting two figures with a familiarity that belied the years since they last stood side-by-side. Agent Smith, the FBI's sharp-eyed investigator, slid into the room, sharp as a tack with eyes like black marbles. His cheekbones were like knives, and his face was chiseled into sharp angles from years of chasing bad guys. Dark hair, once wild, was now slicked back, highlighting the steel in his gaze. His sharp suit barely contained his wiry frame, coiled with hidden power.

A quick grin flashed, showing his comic relief attitude—a ghost of past victories and shared secrets—before his face hardened into focus. This was a street fighter in a fancy suit, an FBI agent ready to crack any case.

Beside him stood Agent Henderson; a human mountain rumbling in like a boulder shifting. His broad shoulders strained against his suit, and each wrinkle told a lengthy tale carrying the nation's secrets. His face, marred by late nights spent breaking codes, held the quiet power of a thunderstorm. His deep blue eyes hid a sharp mind that could see through lies and uncover truths.

He rarely spoke, but when he did, the words boomed. This was a titan of logic and reason, an NSA agent whose mind was a fortress, ready to defend the nation's secrets.

As different as night and day, these two stood together, their past and loyalty forging a bond like steel. A silent nod and a shared glance— an invisible solidarity amid shared dangers—flickered between them.

Years might have separated their paths, but the bedrock of their camaraderie remained as solid as the granite walls that were about to cradle their hushed meeting.

Lt. General Adams' face, imprinted with the weight of the nation's security, broke into a grim smile.

"Gentlemen," he said, his voice low and gravelly, completely at odds with the dull clicking of his heels against the polished floor. "At ease."

The agents settled into their chairs, and faces resembling the general's gravity. This wasn't a social call; the air crackled with unspoken urgency.

Adams cleared his throat, the sound echoing in the hushed room. "Thank you for coming, gentlemen," he began, his gaze steady as he met their eyes. "We have a situation that demands the utmost discretion and your unique skillsets."

Lt. General Adams' eyes flickered towards the agents before he said, "I have always been a patriot, you know. I have a deep love for this country. But these days, how things are going in our nation worries me; the changes are not positive. It is more important than ever that we defend it."

He paused, his jaw clenching; the worry written on his face as visible as the medals adorning his chest. "There are a few I can trust in the government, and I fear that there are individuals in our departments and agencies who may be working against us, trying to tear down the very fabric of this nation."

Agent Smith looked forward with his sharp eyes, elaborating on the general's concern. "General," he said, his voice a steady counterpoint to the turbulence of the room, "you know we'd walk through fire for you. What's bothering you? What's going on?"

Lt. General Adams' voice dropped to a whisper, heavy with the classified knowledge. "A leak, gentlemen. A classified one. Pentagon secrets, whispers of war plans, and cutting-edge tech are finding their way across the Pacific into the hands of the Dragon."

A collective gasp filled the room. Agent Henderson raised an eyebrow in disbelief. "China?"

Lt. General Adams' gaze met his steely resolve. "Yes," he rasped, slamming a file on the table. "Concrete evidence, undeniable proof. This is a threat that damages more than any bomb, gentlemen. It's an attack at our very core, a viper gnawing at the heart of our nation."

Agent Henderson's face hardened; his features grim under the harsh light. "What's the point of all this secrecy?" he asked, his voice carrying in the quiet room. "You know that we are on the same team?"

Adams' face tightened, leaving deeper lines in his aging appearance. "We're the wall, gentlemen," he said, his voice gravelly with the weight of the words. "But this ain't your usual brick-and-mortar job. This requires shadows, not spotlights."

He leaned, in his eyes flashing with a steely glint. "I need a team that is untraceable and discreet. Like ghosts operating outside the grid. These leaks and these stolen documents threaten the nation's very core. We can't afford leaks, not even whispers. This operation doesn't exist, not officially. Are you still with me?"

Smith's jaw clenched; mirroring the general's grim resolve. "Always, General. You point, we dig."

Henderson raised his voice in full approval. "Consider it done."

Adams nodded, a tinge of relief battling the dark circles around his eyes. "Good. Remember, your lips are sealed tighter than a tomb. I'm your only contact, your only lifeline. And just in case, let's say, I've taken precautions. My lawyer holds a failsafe, a dead man's switch. If I go dark, the truth explodes and shines a light on this whole damn operation. It'll protect your ass and keep you out of the fire.

"We'll see this through, General," Henderson's voice thundered.

Adams placed a battered hand on the table, the map of his life etched on its calloused surface. "Thank you, gentlemen. Now, listen closely. I'll lay out what we know. These stolen documents are the tip of a dark iceberg. Classified intelligence, weapons research, and secrets that could topple nations. Someone's feeding them out, piece by piece, like a venomous serpent shedding its skin."

As Adams continued shedding light on the matter, the air in the room grew thicker with each revelation, heavy with the weight of unseen threats and potential devastation.

Agent Smith's voice, barely a whisper, leaned forward, obsidian eyes glinting with grim understanding. "This is bigger than we thought, General," he rasped. "We'll need a team—a hell of a team— to tackle this."

Adams' gaze met Smith's. "Indeed," he rumbled, the nation's weight settling on his broad shoulders. "And you will have every resource at your disposal. But remember Agent; this operation cloaks itself in shadows. There are no official channels, no leaks, and no whispers. This room becomes your genesis, your sanctuary. The outside world remains blissfully ignorant."

A muscle flickered in Henderson's jaw, his imposing frame radiating quiet confidence. "We'll be your silent guardians, General," he murmured, his voice a low rumble that echoed off the sterile walls. "Protecting our nation from the unseen."

Adams nodded, a small flicker of satisfaction sparking in his storm-cloud eyes. "That's the spirit. Now, listen closely. I'll brief you on everything we know so far. Your task is to assemble a team. Ghosts, phantoms, and individuals operating in the gray are untraceable and untouchable. This room is their womb, their confessional. Their loyalty lies not with the flag but with the mission, with America's hidden pulse."

Smith leaned back, his eyes narrowing in concentration. "Understood, General. We start... now."

A grim smile played on Adams' lips. "Good. I knew I could count on you two. Tread carefully, gentlemen. The fate of millions hangs in the balance."

Henderson's gaze, unwavering, met the general's. "We won't fail you, sir."

The classified intelligence was exchanged, a silent pact was forged, and the two agents rose, their footsteps muffled by the thick carpet. The heavy steel door hissed shut, severing their connection to the outside world.

The Silent Guardians were born in that sterile cocoon, stepping into a twilight world full of conspiracy theories and hidden agendas.

Their mission, etched in blood and whispered in shadows, was clear: unmask the unseen enemy, safeguard their nation's secrets, and ensure the truth remained buried even within their own government.

As they strode into the world beyond the secure room, their faces cloaked in shadows; the world remained blissfully unaware of the storm brewing in its midst.

The Silent Guardians had begun their dance—a waltz with danger, a tango with oblivion.

Now, the hunt has commenced. Smith and Henderson, ghosts flitting through the underbelly of society, scoured the fringes for their recruits.

***

Like a curious child, sunlight tiptoed through Dr. Brett Evans' window, casting warm stripes across the worn leather of his armchair. Here, amidst the battlefield of papers and half-eaten cereal, he wrestled with the enigmas of human behavior. His brow furrowed like a well-worn map, hinting at the maze-like roads his mind wandered through.

Crisp blue eyes, flecked with gold like sunlit wheat, were momentarily veiled by thick lashes as he absorbed the latest twist in the case. Under a shock of sun-kissed blonde hair, a hint of worry formed lines around his eyes, presenting the emotional toll his work exacted.

Yet, even though, Dr. Evans was tired, he was determined to keep going. He was a strong-willed person, who was very good at understanding people. He was tall and lean and had worked hard for many years. Dr. Evans always stayed calm, even in difficult situations.

Dr. Evans was an expert at sifting through the complex webs of the human psyche to find the truth. He was a retired LAPD detective, who was now a forensic psychology consultant.

Due to his proficiency in hypnosis, questioning techniques, and polygraph analysis, he was in high demand by law enforcement organizations worldwide. But here, in the silence of his Sherman Oaks haven, he took pleasure in the luxury of digging into cold cases, untangling their knots at his own pace.

The serenity shattered with the sudden jangle of the phone. Dr. Evans straightened, the furrow deepening, as he answered with a practiced calm, "Doctor Evans."

The voice on the other end was the complete opposite of the soft jazz playing in the background. Crisp and authoritative, it sliced through the serene atmosphere like a knife.

"Doctor Evans," the voice said, "this is Agent Smith from the Federal Bureau of Investigation. We just landed in Los Angeles, carrying a matter of national security. We require your expertise immediately."

Dr. Evans' heart skipped a beat. 'National security? This was no run-of-the-mill missing person case,' he thought to himself.

His grip tightened on the phone. "Agent Smith," he said, his voice steady. "Let me know about it when you get here."

The call ended, leaving a tense silence filled with unspoken nervousness. The serene oasis of Dr. Evans' office had transformed into a launch-pad for something far more dangerous. He leaned back, eyes narrowed, the gears of his analytical mind clicking into place.

National security meant lives hung in the balance, secrets whispered in the shadows. And Brett Evans, the man, who walked through the labyrinthine paths of the human mind, was about to be thrust into the heart of a new, high-stakes mystery.

The next thirty minutes stretched like an eternity. The jazz music now felt jarring; its upbeat rhythm counterbalanced the upheaval raging within Dr. Evans.

He paced the room, restless energy crackling around him. Finally, the doorbell's chime was a welcome release, a signal that the dance with the unknown was about to begin.

Dr. Evans rose, his gaze hardening with resolve. He crossed the room and swung the door open, meeting the faces of two men who carried the weight of their mission in their eyes.

Agent Smith, tall and sharp-edged, his gaze as steely as his tailored suit, offered a curt nod. Beside him stood Agent Henderson, a mountain of a man with an intellect that shone even through the controlled intensity of his demeanor.

Agent Smith walked into Dr. Evans' office, urgency crackling in the air like static. Rather than wasting time on small talk, he launched into a terrifying story that made the doctor shudder. The foundation of national security—highly classified documents—had disappeared, possibly falling into the hands of the Chinese government. The leak was a gaping wound, jeopardizing the nation's defense and igniting a cold sweat of panic on Evans' brow.

Dr. Evans, a man forged from composure and razor-sharp intellect, absorbed the details like a sponge. His mind, a machine of logic and deduction, whirred to life, eager to dissect the fragments of this complex puzzle.

The stolen documents were more than just paper; they were weapons that could have caused the country irreversible harm. The stakes were unthinkably high, and the future was uncertain.

"So, what do you need from me?" Evans asked, his voice steady but betraying a simmering sense of impending doom.

Agent Henderson, the stoic mountain beside Smith, cleared his throat. "Public trust in the Justice Department is shot," he said, his voice heavy with a weight that wasn't his own. "They see it as a political weapon, not a protector."

Evans raised an eyebrow; skepticism flickering in his eyes. "And how does that concern me?"

"We can't unleash our own agents on the Capitol," Henderson explained, his words measured. "Asking questions of high-ranking officials, poking around classified shadows... it'd be a political firestorm."

Smith leaned forward, his gaze like a laser; "That's where you come in, Doc. We need your help prying the truth from under its rock."

Intrigued by the challenge and the weight of responsibility, Evans sat up straighter. "And what, precisely, would my role be?"

Henderson met his gaze, hoping to illuminate his weathered face. "We need your unique skillset, Doc. Your interviews that peel back layers like an onion, your interrogations that crack even the toughest shells, your hypnotic dives into hidden memories, your polygraph that separates truth from lies like wheat from chaff. We need a new set of eyes—someone who can navigate the Capitol's corridors without setting off alarms."

A faint smile played on Evans' lips. The task was perilous and fraught with unseen dangers, but the chance to serve his country, and to be the unseen shield against a silent threat ignited a fire in his soul.

He leaned back in his chair, a glint of steel in his eyes. "Alright, gentlemen. Tell me everything."

Once filled with nervous tension, the room crackled with new energy—the excitement of purpose, of a shared mission born out of the fires of necessity.

The nation's fate hung in the balance, and Dr. Evans, the unassuming hero, was their last and best hope. The hunt for the stolen documents, a dance with shadows and secrets, had just begun.

Dr. Evans' pulse quickened. Not with fear, though the case file hummed with danger and complexity. No, this was the buzz of the chase, the thrill of the hunt.

His mind, a finely honed instrument, vibrated with the prospect of finding his way through the tangled knot of secrets before him. Mysteries had always been his siren song—the challenge of peeling back layers of deception and finding the truth beneath. This espionage case surrounding stolen documents was an anthem to his intellectual prowess.

"I'm in," he declared, voice firm, the decision not a question but a resolute step into the unknown.

Chapter Two:
The Nexus Unveiled

Dr. Brett Evans was suddenly yanked from his quiet life and dropped into a top-secret government facility in Washington, D.C.

Rain lashed against the windshield as Agent Brett pulled into the nondescript parking lot. Tucked away on the D.C. outskirts, the building looked more like a sleepy office block than a state-of-the-art government facility. But appearances, as Brett knew well, could be deceiving. This nondescript shell housed "The Nexus," the top-secret nerve center for the elite federal task force, bringing together the best minds of the FBI and NSA.

He stepped out into the downpour, the cold air biting at his cheeks. The facility's existence in Washington was unknown, but it was self-sufficient and equipped with state-of-the-art technology and advanced security measures. It was converted specifically for this special task force's use.

Agent Henderson and a few other agents greeted Brett as he pushed open the heavy doors of the hidden back room.

"Brett." Agent Henderson greeted him, his handshake firm and familiar. "Let me introduce you to our team."

"Alright, listen up," Henderson boomed his voice echoing in the hushed room.

"That's John Carter," he declared, pointing to a figure sitting around the round table. "John has a background in computer science and is an experienced FBI agent. For anything related to cybersecurity, he is the expert. He is incredibly knowledgeable about digital forensics, encryption, and hacking. His objective is essential for locating risks and following up on electronic leads."

Henderson's finger pointed next to a woman sitting beside John Carter.

"Agent Sarah Miller," he announced. "Sarah's area of expertise is cryptanalysis. She is an FBI veteran with a special knack for deciphering codes and ciphers. Her remarkable aptitude for deciphering intricate communications and encryption schemes comes in handy when interacting with covert groups."

Brett's gaze flickered to a figure pouring a steaming cup of coffee. "That's Special Agent Mark Ramirez. Tactical Operations. Mark is a former member of the Navy SEAL. He brings his elite tactical training to the team. His expertise in field operations, combat, and counterterrorism makes him an indispensable asset during high-risk missions. He's known for his level-headedness under pressure." Henderson rumbled, his voice tinged with respect.

Finally, Henderson gestured towards a woman with nimble fingers flying across a keyboard. "Dr. Emily Chang," he introduced. "Emily was recruited from the NSA as a linguistic enigma skilled at reading body language and hidden messages spoken in foreign tongues. Her ability to crack the code of human communication, both spoken and unspoken, is an invaluable asset in the murky world of international espionage."

Undeterred, Agent Smith, ever-focused, wasted no time on pleasantries. He asked Brett and Henderson to follow him. They went into a small room away from the team, where Agent Smith laid out the mission with the precision of a surgeon's scalpel.

"Evans," he began, leaning forward, "We have your cover identification ready. You will be a 'Personnel Evaluation Manager.' Your mission is to access federal buildings, departments, and agencies all over D.C., investigating for stolen documents and data theft."

Evans, unflinching under the weight of expectations, let out a low chuckle. "Higher positions, bigger paychecks," he mused. "I'm sure that no one will turn down a chat with a friendly evaluator."

The trio returned to the main room, and Henderson gathered the team close. Dr. Brett Evans stepped through the threshold, drawing curious glances from the assembled team.

"Hey, people. Listen up. This is Doctor Evans, our final member of this team." He announced, gesturing to Evans. Some of you may already know him. Maybe you have worked with him in the past. Evans will be working mostly on his own, coordinating with us on a frequent basis. If he calls in or contacts any of you, asking for your help, please assist in any way you can. Any questions?"

A ripple of murmurs, laced with intrigue, swept through the room. Everyone knew the gravity of their mission, and Evans' arrival signaled a step into the unknown.

No questions, no hesitations. Just a chorus of nods, eyes steeled with silent commitment.

Brett then, waved to all the team in the room. "Thank you. Nice to meet all of you."

Dr. Evans quickly adjusted in his makeshift war room. Time was a luxury they didn't possess. The stolen documents, containing classified national security secrets, had vanished like smoke, leaving behind a trail of suspicion and unease. Brett, however, was no stranger to chasing ghosts.

His eyes, sharp as a hawk's, scanned through a mountain of files, piecing together fragments of information like a master puzzle builder. Each interview, each interrogation, was a delicate chess game. He studied every flicker of a suspect's gaze and every nervous tick, decoding the subtle language of the body that often betrayed what the lips refused to confess.

But the stolen documents were just the tip of the iceberg. The real prize lay buried deeper, hidden within the endless tunnels of the subconscious. With a practiced hand, Brett ventured into the area of forensic hypnosis, a tool as delicate as a scalpel and as dangerous as a tightrope walk.

His days were a blur of strategy sessions, intel analysis, and covert communication with the task force team. As a self-proclaimed "Personnel Evaluation Manager," he built an elaborate web of carefully constructed lies, infiltrating federal agencies one by one. Fake badges sat nestled in his pocket, a fabricated backstory that protected him against scrutiny. His charm, a honed weapon, disarmed unsuspecting officials, granting him access to restricted files and whispered conversations.

Weeks bled into months, the pressure mounting with each passing day. Under the confident facade, Brett, the hunter, became the hunted. Every glance, every interaction, held the potential for exposure.

***

One of the first stops was at the Department of Justice. Its halls echoed with Brett's confident strides. Badge flashing, he introduced himself as a "Personal Evaluation Manager," his eyes glinting with a practiced smile. Eager for advancement, the employees spilled their guts about the agency's inner workings and whispered about classified projects. Each visit to another department or agency was a dive into a web of secrets, with Brett surfacing with dripping clues and a growing map of the government's hidden veins.

Weeks blurred into a whirlwind of meetings, briefings, and late-night analysis with the task force. Every lead Brett unearthed, every hushed rumor gleaned from a nervous bureaucrat, was thoroughly verified. Meanwhile, the task force team continued a parallel investigation, cross-referencing information and following potential leads he discovered.

One weary evening, after sifting through the Department of Homeland Security's cryptic data, Brett returned to his Spartan apartment to find an encrypted message shimmering on his screen. Agent Smith's words were cryptic, hinting at a shadowy organization called "The Hydra," with tentacles reaching the highest government ranks. This was it! He'd been searching for this missing piece.

Dawn found Brett pacing the war room, briefing the team with a grim urgency. The air trembled under the weight of his revelation: high-ranking officials, whose names were whispered with awe and fear, were implicated in the thefts.

Henderson, with his sharp eyes scanning the faces around the table, spoke with the quiet authority of a seasoned soldier. "This is a turning point, gentlemen. We tread in viper's nest territory now. One wrong move, one careless whisper, and everything unravels. Brett's lead points to the beast's heart, but we need to operate with the precision of a scalpel. No missteps, no heroes. Just cold, calculated action."

The room fell silent, the gravity of their situation pressing down on each member. They were no longer chasing ghosts; they were staring into the abyss, and the abyss, it seemed, stared back.

Agent Smith's steely gaze met Brett's across the cluttered desk.

"Brett," Smith's voice was low and gravelly, each word punctuated by the tap of his pen against the report. "Brett, you've done a great job so far, but now the challenge begins. We need to expose "The Hydra" and ensure their influence is eradicated."

Brett's voice was a low rumble, each word etched with grim resolve: "I'm ready. We have a lot of work ahead of us."

Chapter Three:
Unveiling The Underbelly

Agent Smith's words hung heavy in the air, amplifying the tension. Brett, his eyes like smoldering embers, stared at the report on his desk, its pages filled with coded messages and cryptic diagrams—a map to dismantling "The Hydra."

He knew the stakes. The hidden network had burrowed deep within the government, its tendrils reaching into every corner of power. To expose them, meant facing an enemy who was invisible, ruthless, and infinitely dangerous.

Sleep became a luxury, he couldn't afford. Coffee fueled his nights, and the bitter taste on his tongue constantly reminded him of the truth he was chasing. His apartment morphed into a war room, with walls plastered with maps, notes, and scribbled theories. He devoured every lead and every scrap of information, and his mind was a frantic puzzle box, piecing together the larger picture.

One night, as exhaustion gnawed at his bones and shadows danced on the dark room's ceiling, a notification pinged on his laptop screen. An anonymous email, devoid of a subject line, with just a single chilling sentence: "Look into the hidden rooms beneath the Capitol."

His blood turned to ice. The cryptic email was gone in the blink of an eye, as it had never been in the inbox. But it had burrowed into Brett's mind like a burr under the saddle. Sleep vanished from his eyes, which were burning with the phantom glow of the screen where the message had taunted him. He couldn't afford to dismiss it, not with Hydra's shadow lurking closely around him.

His investigation started not with shovels and crowbars but with books and discretion. The Capitol's history was filled with hidden spaces and dusty conspiracies passed down from architect to historian. He went through the accounts of secret meetings, clandestine escapes, and forgotten chambers. Some dismissed them as folklore, others as embellished history. But for Brett, each tale was a piece of the puzzle; a light at the end of the tunnel.

His official cover as "Personnel Evaluation Manager" became his Trojan horse. He interviewed senators and representatives, their voices a chorus of guarded whispers and feigned ignorance. Yet, Brett saw cracks in their facades in the flicker of an eye, a knowing glance, or a nervous cough. He learned of hushed conversations in "ancient nooks"—doors hidden behind unmarked passageways leading to the bowels of the building.

Brett's pursuit of the truth had become a relentless tide, washing away any semblance of normalcy in his life. His apartment devolved into a makeshift archive stacked with dusty tomes, cryptic maps, and dog-eared research papers. The flickering light of his computer screen devoured the nights as his eyes combed through digital files and old archives.

His interviews, conducted under the guise of "Personnel Evaluation Manager," took on a new dimension. He honed his skills in subtle hypnosis, planting seeds of suggestion that coaxed out forgotten memories and whispered rumors from even the most tight-lipped officials. The fragmented and cryptic stories spoke of generations-old secrets and hushed exchanges in dimly lit chambers beneath the Capitol's polished facade.

One fateful day at the National Archives, a faded blueprint hidden within a forgotten file sent a jolt through Brett. It depicted a labyrinthine network of tunnels and concealed rooms, each carefully labeled with cryptic symbols, and archaic titles. The whispers, he'd heard were no longer just folklore; they were a visible map, an invitation into the very heart of the hidden government.

His fingers trembled as he traced the lines of the blueprint, a thrill of anticipation battling with a gnawing fear. He knew that this was a pivotal moment, a crossroads between pursuit and peril.

With a committed attitude, Brett went after a meeting with Mr. Anderson, the retired archivist who was the first to make the suggestion about the hidden network.

They met at a coffee shop. The smoky aroma of espresso danced with the mellow tune of a jazz saxophone as Brett approached Mr. Anderson's table. He had discovered the name of another retired archivist in a remote section of the internet where rumors of old-fashioned conspiracies and mysterious cabals were common. Pretending to be that person, Earl Parker, who was an authority on the fringe, Brett posed as a self-proclaimed connoisseur of the fringe.

"Mr. Anderson, a pleasure!" Brett's voice was a touch too eager, a practiced enthusiasm honed from years of experience.

"Mr. Parker, good evening." Mr. Anderson shook hands with Brett as they both took a seat. Brett got down to business.

"I stumbled upon your article on the Illuminati influence in the Library of Congress – fascinating stuff, by the way!"

Anderson, a wisp of a man with eyes that held the glint of forgotten tales, smiled wryly. "Ah, the Illuminati. Still drawing a crowd, even after all these years."

Their conversation spiraled deeper, a conspiratorial ballet of ifs and maybes. They dissected government files for hidden codes, analyzed cryptic symbols on ancient statues, and debated the plausibility of alien contact under the guise of UFO sightings. Brett, all wide eyes and feigned skepticism, listened intently, soaking up Anderson's every word.

As they sipped their drinks, they struck up a conversation about their shared love for books. The coffee shop buzzed with the aroma of freshly brewed coffee and the sound of soft jazz playing in the background.

Brett leaned forward, his eyes glinting with a calculated spark. "Mr. Anderson, your information about the history of the National Archives is appreciated, but you mentioned something about hidden rooms beneath the Capitol. Can you elaborate on that?"

The weathered man, his eyes twinkling with a knowing glint; listened intently as Brett laid out his findings.

"The blueprints," Anderson rasped, his voice like dry leaves rustling in the wind, "It's not common knowledge, just rumors, but there are chambers beneath the Capitol. They date back to the founding of this country. Some say, they hold the key to untold secrets."

Anderson leans in closer and whispers, "Some even believe, they're linked to a hidden network within the government, a group that's pulling the strings from behind the scenes."

After the meeting ended, Brett was driving back to his apartment. As he navigated through the busy city streets, Brett couldn't help but reflect on the important discussion that took place during the meeting. The weight of his responsibilities lingered in his mind, reminding him of the challenges that lay ahead. But he was more determined than ever, mumbling to himself, "I need to know more. I believe, I've stumbled upon something here."

Chapter Four: Chambers Of Power

Brett pressed on with the investigation process, sifting through mountains of classified documents. Each layer peeled back, revealing another whisper of "The Hydra," a clandestine network manipulating world events from the shadows of the Capitol. Letters hinted at hidden chambers and vaults brimming with secrets that fueled an invisible empire. "Deep state," he muttered, the term tasting bitter on his tongue.

Just as another dead end threatened to swallow him whole, the phone buzzed. A raspy whisper sliced through the silence, "Evans, you got the email, haven't you? Look into the hidden rooms beneath the Capitol." The cryptic message from his elusive source sent a jolt through him.

"Yes, I did," Brett breathed back, "Who are you? Why are you sending me this tip?"

"I can't reveal my identity," the voice hissed hesitantly, "but I can tell you this- those chambers are real. They hold the secrets of power that have been hidden for centuries."

Brett's stomach clenched. "I'm listening."

"You need to find the blueprints and the maps," the source urged, their voice laced with urgency. "They'll guide you to the truth. But be careful, Evans. This path risks your life."

The words hung heavy as Brett hung up. His hunt for the buried chambers intensified. One rain-soaked night, he stumbled upon a little bar tucked away in the quieter corners of Washington, D.C. Known for its history-loving patrons, the establishment was the kind of place where whispered secrets between friends took on a life of their own. While nursing his drink, he caught a fragment of a hushed conversation at the next table.

"I heard they have found a secret room beneath the Capitol," a man leaned in conspiratorially.

"Hidden room? What's in it?" the other rasped.

"The rumor is that it contains priceless historical documents hidden away from the public eye. But it's all highly confidential, you understand?"

Brett's pulse quickened. This was it, the lead he'd been chasing. He inched closer, ears burning, soaking up every morsel of the clandestine conversation. The hunt for the truth, for The Hydra's hidden lair, had just taken a sharp turn into the heart of the lion's den.

"I know a guy," the first man leaned in further, "Used to work at the National Archives for 30 years. He's retired now, but he probably knows more about the Capitol and its secrets than anyone in Washington."

Brett's heart hammered. This was his shot. The men finished their hushed exchange, and Brett, stomach churning with nerves, approached.

"Excuse me," Brett began, voice steady despite his racing pulse, "I couldn't help but overhear your conversation. I am a historian, and I am deeply curious about this hidden room under the Capitol. Can you help me get in touch with your contact from the National Archives?"

The man eyed Brett, suspicion lingering. Finally, a curt nod. "Meet me here tomorrow at the same time. I'll see what I can do."

The next day, back in the smoky bar, Brett was introduced to Mr. Lawrence Montgomery, the retired National Archives employee/whisperer. A tall, wiry man in his late sixties with silver hair, and a stern demeanor, Montgomery's gaze held the weight of countless secrets.

"My friend told me you were a historian." His voice rumbled, curiosity battling caution. "I am happy to share information with historians who are on a quest to uncover history's secrets."

Brett, understanding the gravity of their pact, nodded fervently. Montgomery's hand extended, offering a worn diary and an aged map.

"These will be your guides," he said, his eyes glinting. "But be warned, the journey will be treacherous. The entrance to the hidden chambers beneath the Capitol is a well-guarded secret. Follow the directions in the diary and the map, and remember to tread lightly."

The diary, its pages' brittle with time, held the key. Intricate passages, hidden doors, cryptic symbols etched into the Capitol's very walls, a whispered map leading to a buried truth. The accompanying map, a detailed blueprint, revealed the chambers' location and their connection to the Capitol's grand facade.

Brett's fingers trembled as he traced the lines. He would tread lightly, yes, but he wouldn't back down. The hidden chambers awaited, and with them, the potential to shatter the very foundation of power.

The game was in full swing.

The next morning, Brett clutched the diary and map, his heart pounding with anticipation. He entered the Capitol building, blending seamlessly with the throngs of tourists. Each step felt like a pilgrimage, tracing the footsteps of giants, who have had shaped the nation's history.

The diary's cryptic instructions led him on a labyrinthine path, doubling back on himself, and squeezing through narrow passageways. He soon realized, he was navigating a hidden network beneath the Capitol, a maze of chambers and tunnels guarded by ingenious traps and intricate puzzles.

As Brett ventured deeper into the Capitol, he encountered unexpected obstacles. His mind raced as he deciphered ancient symbols etched into the marble, revealing hidden switches that unlocked secret doors. He held his breath, tiptoeing across pressure-sensitive floor tiles, the threat of alarms a constant companion.

Days bled into nights as Brett meticulously followed the diary's whispers. Each dawn found him back in the Capitol, adrenaline coursing through his veins as he dodged security patrols and eluded watchful cameras. He was a ghost in a grand monument, his every move a calculated gamble.

Exhaustion gnawed at him, the Capitol's immensity a cruel reminder of the secrets it held close. Finally, after what felt like an eternity, he reached a dead-end corridor. The diary fell silent; its final clue was a cryptic note scrawled on the worn page.

With a surge of desperation, Brett pressed a seemingly unremarkable stone on the wall. The world lurched, a section of the wall grinding aside to reveal a gaping maw. He stepped into the darkness, his senses overwhelmed by the musty air and the immensity of the hidden space beneath the Capitol.

The passage opened into a vast chamber, its walls adorned with faded murals depicting forgotten chapters of history. In the center, a pedestal held a tarnished object, its surface glinting with an otherworldly light. Brett's breath caught in his throat as he realized he had stumbled upon a secret buried deep within the heart of the nation.

Brett's phone flashlight sliced through the dust motes dancing in the stagnant air as he recorded everything through his phone's camera. Walls of books, row upon row, stretched into the shadows, their leather spines whispering forgotten tales. Parchment crackled as his gloved fingers skimmed brittle documents, each yellowed scroll a time capsule waiting to be pried open. Days bled into nights as Brett meticulously documented his finds. Priceless treaties, handwritten manifestos, faded maps—the history of a nation slumbered here, undisturbed for centuries.

Then, a revelation tucked behind a leather-bound tome, a diary. Ink faded with time, but the scrawled words still thrummed with urgency. A senator's secret musings, laying bare the Capitol's underbelly, its whispers of corruption and conspiracy. Excitement snaked through Brett's veins. More diaries followed, journals filled with incriminating confessions, whispered plans, and hidden agendas. Each page is a brushstroke painting of a portrait of a city fueled by secrets.

With trembling hands, Brett selected a handful of documents. These weren't merely historical relics; they were keys. Keys to unlocking the conspiracy, exposing the rot at the heart of the nation. A hushed whisper escaped his lips, "These documents are one more step to the key that may unravel the entire conspiracy."

Brett's eyes, gleaming with newfound purpose, darted through the labyrinthine shelves. This wasn't just a hidden chamber; it was a war room, a crucible where truth would be forged from the ashes of decades of lies. And he, the unlikely warrior armed with whispers from the past, was ready to take the fight to the shadows.

Brett's heart hammered against his ribs as he inched through the shadows, the incriminating files tucked tight against his waistband. He'd ghosted through the labyrinthine chambers, his eyes scanning every corner for pursuers, but now, the distant echo of footsteps sent a jolt of panic through him. He wasn't alone.

He lunged behind a towering stack of dusty tomes, the air thick with the musty scent of forgotten knowledge. From his vantage point, he watched a group of grim-faced security personnel, led by a woman with eyes like flint, flood into the chamber.

"We've received an anonymous tip about an intruder in the hidden rooms," the woman barked, her voice echoing through the hushed halls. "Search the area thoroughly. We can't let this breach of security go unpunished."

Brett's breath hitched in his throat. The diary and map, his only hope of exposing the conspiracy, were burning against his skin. He had to get out now.

He retraced his steps, his mind racing through the maze of hidden passageways etched in his memory. The diary and map, his tattered guides, led him on a desperate dance through the Capitol's underbelly. He dodged security patrols, his every move a calculated gamble against the ticking clock.

Finally, a narrow staircase, barely a crack in the ancient stone, offered a glimmer of hope. He clambered up, the footsteps below fading with each step. The stairs spat him out into a nondescript corridor, the Capitol's bustling thrum a stark contrast to the tense silence he'd left behind.

With a final, fleeting glance back at the hidden chambers, Brett melted into the crowd, the weight of his secret a heavy cloak on his shoulders. He knew the secrets that he carried could topple empires, but first, he had to survive.

Once safely back in his apartment war room, he takes out the stolen documents and examines them more closely. Brett placed a crucial call to Agent Smith. "I may have some of the documents, we've been looking for, Smith. This is a breakthrough," he growled, "I suggest you assemble the team right away. We need to analyze the documents for fingerprints and possible DNA."

Smith's voice crackled through the receiver, urgency leaching into it. "Meet at the Elm Street warehouse. Abandoned; secure."

Darkness clung to the warehouse like a second skin as Brett and Smith met, flashlights carving thin beams through the gloom. Documents, weighty with secrets, passed from hand to hand. "Smith, handle them carefully," Brett rasped, "These documents could expose the mutts and their nefarious activities."

***

At Nexus, the team devoured the documents. Days blurred into nights as they meticulously analyzed every smudge, every fingerprint, every whisper of DNA.

Brett knew returning to the hidden rooms was a gamble that he couldn't afford. Instead, he retreated, his mind a whirlwind of information. The documents whispered of the Capitol's hidden history about the United States. Exposing it now could unravel everything.

Weeks bled into one another as Brett meticulously categorized his discoveries. He contacted NSA Agent Henderson, voice tight with urgency. "Henderson, I need our team to help me decipher and authenticate the historical documents and artifacts and separate them from any official documents pertaining to our investigation."

Henderson's response was swift, a lifeline thrown across the chasm of uncertainty. "We can do that, Brett. Get them over to our operations center, and we'll get started."

Chapter Five:
Shadows Beneath The Capitol

Senator Monroe, one of the lone rangers amongst the suits and the smiles that inhabited the Senate, slunk through marbled corridors before Brett and the 'NEXUS' task force canvassed down the details of HYDRA's investigation. Whispers of scandal scrawled the map of his mind, a conspiracy reeking of backroom deals and dirty cash. He played one-man intel operation for months, peeling away the layers like a bad onion. He would pile evidence, stinking and growing, on his ad hoc palace of truth.

He knew, the hammer wouldn't tap; it'd roar. Careers would splinter like dropped china, dissolving reputations like sugar in water. Was this a carefully staged political play? Dust in the wind. He saw those faces: senators with greasy smiles and eyes like poker chips, lobbyists dripping oil, and, worst of all, a couple of names close enough to call friends.

But exposure, the earth-shaking kind, wasn't the finish line. Monroe craved justice—the real deal, not some gavel's hollow clang. He was dealing with the desire to rip the mask off this nest of vipers and expose the rot like a surgeon under harsh lights. This wasn't the semblance of a search for truths; it was a combat against the shadows suffocating the city.

Heavily weighed down by it all, an icy leaden cloak chills his spine. He knew, they watched—the vipers he was about to uncoil. But fear? It was not ice; it was fuel. In chess, he played against fire-breathing dragons; every step was a gamble with the neck on the tutorial line.

He didn't have much time left; he was a ticking bomb, and the noose was tightening. He had one shot; that's all. He had one shot to bathe the city in the unforgiving light of the truth. Senator Monroe, the lone wolf, howled at the hoard of dragons, ready to pounce.

One evening, a note crumpled and scrawled in jittery handwriting hid within the hidden pockets of the Senate office room. For Senator Monroe, a weathered oak amidst polished mahogany, it felt as if ice had crawled down his spine as he began to read it. It was a viper's hiss, a map to a den of corruption that snaked through the heart of power.

Monroe kept his face a stoic mask, but his gut churned. He knew that playing this game alone was a death sentence. He needed eyes, ears, and fangs.

The first choice was Sarah Mitchell, a sharp-tongued aide. As a Personal Assistant, her loyalty was iron, and her mind was a steel trap.

"Sarah," he rasped; jamming the note into her hand. "I need you deeper in the weeds than ever before. We're stepping into a pit of vipers."

Sarah's eyes narrowed, and flickers of fear battled with resolve. "I'm in, Senator. But we'll need one more. Maybe Alex."

"That Ivy League dropout?" Monroe raised an eyebrow at that suggestion.

"Who forced that kid to drop out?" Sarah retorted

Senator Monroe sighed. "What was I supposed to do? How was I supposed to tell everyone that my dead best friend's son hacked into the Pentagon?" Senator Monroe pinched his nose bridge, "Just because he wanted to have fun."

"I know, but he was 15 then. He is 23 years old now."

Senator Monroe couldn't help but agree.

The next aide was Alex Turner, son of the late Senator Will Turner. Alex was a tech wizard, whose mind could break the codes without even trying. He was very much the ghost in the machine and the one who could traverse down the grubby backstreets of the digital world.

"Alex," Monroe said, laying out the grim picture, "we need eyes in the shadows. Can you find the bones these snakes are hiding?"

"Look how tables have turned." Alex joked.

"God damn it." Senator Monroe said through gritted teeth, "This non-serious behavior of his is gonna kill me before the others."

Sarah sighed, and calmed the senator down by saying two magical words, "Alex, focus."

Alex's brow furrowed, his fingers twitching like spiders on a web. "I can try, Senator. But these guys are good. They've got layers of encryption thicker than a politician's lies."

Let's just say once things were sorted out between Alex and Senator Monroe, they started to see eye to eye.

Their meetings were hushed whispers in smoke-filled rooms, a constant dance of fear and determination. Sarah relayed intercepted messages with white knuckles for worry and tight lips for determination. Alex delivered details with a face drawn and pale instead of the usual blue glow from his screen—deleted files, encrypted conversations.

And as he spoke, the stoic oak, Monroe, felt the cracks spreading across his own façade. The weight of their investigation is pressing him down—a suffocating cloak woven with secrets and shadows. But he mustn't falter. The vipers had to be exposed; their fangs were pulled.

This was not a game anymore. It transformed itself into a war, in somber whispers and flickering displays—an attack on the very essence of the institution that they had all sworn to safeguard. And with it, the trinity built in the crucible of fear and faith would be ready for their quiet tempest.

Roars turned into murmurs. Monroe's war room, a cramped oasis in the political hurricane, hummed with a frantic dance of evidence. Every transaction is a digital vine snaking its way back to the same poisoned root—a web of corruption so vast that it casts a shadow over the Capitol itself. Monroe's office door slammed shut, the echo bouncing off the overflowing binders and coffee-stained files. Sarah Mitchell, normally picture-post perfect in keeping her composure, paced like a caged lioness, her fingers gnawing.

"They're blocking us at every turn!" She spat on the floor, throwing a tablet on the desk. "The Rothman deal just vanished from every official record, replaced with clean files."

Monroe slumped into his chair, the granite exterior chipped by fissures of concern. The web that they'd been weaving, tracing threads of illicit funds from obscure shell companies to opulent mansions, had hit a snag—a thick, lawyer-spun wall.

"We need leverage," he rasped, rubbing his temples. "Something concrete, something that they can't bury."

And then, suddenly, there was a form at the window—Alex Turner as a grim reaper in a rumpled suit. "Got it," he rasped, his eyes glinting with predator's excitement. "Bugs in Senator Harris' office picked up juicy calls. He's meeting with Blackstone tonight, the puppet master behind the whole damn show."

A jolt of adrenaline surged through Sarah. "Tonight? We can't risk another leak or another vanishing act. We need to be there."

Monroe's angry fist slammed onto the desk. "Too risky." He emphasized each word with a slap. "Harris is paranoid, and Blackstone... he's a viper with fangs. Getting caught means..."

The heavy threat hung in the air, unspoken. The war that they were waging was a dance on razor blades, each step a gamble with their careers, and their lives.

"No," said Sarah, her voice now hardening with a steely resolve in the face of opposition. "Then I go alone. I can blend it and get close enough to record the conversation. You two stay here; keep up the pressure on the legal front."

A tense silence filled the room. The silent plea and warning were locked in Monroe's gaze along with Sarah's. He knew of the danger and potential for traps. Yet her spirit and unwavering determination mirrored his own.

"Alright," he muttered; his voice hard. "But if something goes wrong, you disappear. Vanish like a ghost, Sarah. Don't let them get their talons into you."

A flicker of fear kindled in Sarah's eyes, quickly snuffed out by a resolute fire. She gave a curt nod, the weight of their clandestine mission settling on her shoulders like a leaden cloak.

The night stretched ahead, a maelstrom of uncertainty.

As Sarah lapsed off the radar, Monroe and Alex stayed in the eye of the storm; their war room was flooded with the harsh glare of computer screens, their faces chiseled with worry, and their hearts pounding a drumbeat of expectancy and fear. The chase was over, and the prey was boxed into a corner. But would they be the ones to deliver the killing blow, or would they fall beside many others in the snake pit?

***

Through the window, the sun lowered itself on the late afternoon sky and cast long shadows inside the office, illuminating stripes of harsh light and cold shadows on the senator's desk. Monroe, along with his mounting dread, traced the worn leather cover of his diary, a silent talisman against the maelstrom brewing within. Each meticulous entry held a truth uncovered; a layer of corruption was peeled to reveal the rotten core inside. It weighed upon him; a year-long investigation pressed into his shoulders like the burden's yolk, suffocating him with a reek of malfeasance.

"This begins tonight," he muttered. The vow in his mouth tasted of ashes.

The door creaked open, and there was Sarah, his shadow and co-conspirator. Her eyes, usually cool pools of calculation, mirrored the flicker of fear and determination twisting in his gut. "Ready?" she whispered, with her voice barely audible over the rumble of distant thunder.

Monroe swallowed, the lump in his throat unmoving. "Almost." He fumbled through the diary, stopping at a particular page. "The evidence. We need to make sure it lives on whatever happens."

Sarah's jaw clenched, her gaze hardening like steel. "Double-encrypted, triple-locked," she rasped. "Only us. Only you and I know where it lies."

A flicker of unease registered in Monroe's face, but only for the briefest of moments before it was masked behind grim resolve. "Good. Because what we're about to unveil will shake this city down to its core. Hell, to the core of the entire damn nation."

He slammed shut the diary, and finality rang in the sound to echo a tense silence. Threats hung unspoken in the air, and every word said, was pressed down with the full weight of their actions as a physical force. Tonight, they walked into the lion's den armed with nothing but the truth as their weapon. The line between hero and martyr had never been thinner.

"Let's go," Sarah said, and her voice was tight with suppressed fear. "It's time somebody showed them what happens when you mess with fire."

They stepped outside the office, a storm brooding outward and in. Overhead, thunder rolled with echoing uncertainty in their hearts. They were David facing Goliath, a pebble against a mountain. Not tonight; tonight, they would not throw that pebble. Tonight, they will be launching a goddamn avalanche.

The drive to where they were headed was a blur of nervous energy and whispered conversation. Her knuckles on the steering wheel were white, and her eyes were darting back and forth in the rearview mirror with keen awareness. Monroe sat beside her, a statue carved from ice, his face betraying nothing of the churning emotions within.

Both walked inside the large building holding their target and sensed the air growing heavy with tension. Monroe adjusted his hidden camera on his lapel, a cold comfort against the vipers he was to face.

"Remember," she hissed, above nothing more than a whisper. "No heroics. Just do as you told me and get out."

Monroe nodded, a curt acknowledgment sealing their shared pact. This was a dance on razor blades, a game of shadows and secrets where one wrong step could mean everything. They stepped into the lion's den with a silent prayer and steely resolve to let go of a storm that had been brewing for one year.

With that, Sarah drove away, leaving Senator Monroe behind. The fate of a nation hung in the balance, and only they were brave or foolish enough to hold it in their trembling hands.

In a hidden basement of a ratty apartment building, Sarah's leg was bouncing, and her eyes were focused on a flickering TV screen in a hidden basement. Alex is chewing his nails after taking hours to edit

Monroe's speech while sitting at an apartment located in a different part of town.

"Ready?" Sarah said in the earpiece. Her voice was tight, like a coiled spring.

The tension in the conference room crackled with electricity. Monroe took a deep breath, feeling the weight of a nation on his shoulders. On the verge of saying something that could send shockwaves, he was about to drop a bomb—not on the senators themselves but in their very midst. This was live ammunition, and by all accounts, the fallout could be explosive.

"As ready as I'll ever be," he mumbled, adjusting his tie.

Monroe played according to the rules; he knew the best way to reveal something was to hold a press conference.

Flashbulbs exploded, each prong projecting the room into a strobe frenzy. A sea of microphones jutted out, its lens a hungry eye waiting to devour the story. Monroe strode onto the podium, a lone figure against the clamor of clicks and murmurs.

He looked around the room, meeting the stares of reporters, the sneering smirks of political rivals, and the worried glances of allies. In his heart, he knew it was done and dusted. This was the point of not reversing.

He cleared his throat; silently crackling.

"Ladies and gentlemen," he began his speech, his voice unshaken despite the tremor in his hands. "I stand before you today not to make accusations but to shed light on the darkness that has festered for too long within the very heart of our democracy."

The room fell silent. Each ear seemed attuned to the sound of his voice, while each eye stayed glued to Monroe. He paused for a second or two in order to let the full implications of his words sink in.

They had only just begun fighting for their democracy.

A reporter leaned forward, eyes gleaming. "Mr. Monroe, can you be more specific? What darkness are you referring to?"

Monroe replied, his voice carrying hints of steel, "There are whispers in the wind, shadows flitting through the corridors of power. Whispers of deals struck in the dead of night, of favors traded in gilded rooms beneath the very dome of this nation."

The other reporter, from another tabloid known for its sensationalistic reporting, jumped in and said, "Are you intimating corruption, Mr. Monroe? Are you imputing evil to presently serving senators?"

Monroe leveled a gaze at him. "I am not here to say names, gentlemen. But I urge you to listen closely to the whispers and to follow the shadows. The truth, like a stubborn weed, always finds a crack in the pavement."

The tension in the room cracked.

Cameras clicked, and flashbulbs exploded. Monroe, serene amidst the storm, continued, "This is not about politics. This is about accountability. This is all about making sure those who hold the levers of power serve not their own interests but the interests of the people whose mandate they swore to protect and sustain.

One final question: this was from a very young, idealistic reporter with fire in her eyes. "Mr. Monroe, what do we, the press, have the power to do to help shine light into this darkness?"

Monroe smiled, and hope flickered in his eyes. "Shine your light, young lady. Shine it bright. Be the hounds of truth, fat and full, and chase justice on the back of lies. The people deserve to know, and it is you, the press, who hold the key to unlocking the truth."

With that, Monroe walked backward in a supple stride with all those lights across the world of buzz into new lights altogether, into scenes of choice and elegance. And the press, armed by his words and their insatiable curiosity, fanned out through the night and became ravenous to trail shadows and hunt wolves.

Sarah watched the press conference on her laptop. She smiled knowingly, more like a leader than an assassin. It had all begun with Monroe, and she, along with the press, would see that the flames were not doused until shadows were devoured in their fire. Files flitted through the shadows of the internet like poisoned darts, landing anonymously in the hungry mailboxes of journalists. Press, pack of feral hounds hungry for blood.

Senators, once arrogant wolves, are now whimpering under the public's hungry gaze. Sarah's face was painted with worry lines, thrown in stark relief by the flickering glow of her laptop as she watched Monroe's press conference.

Beads of sweat had formed on his forehead, and his voice bounced off the walls like steel as he exposed the rotten belly of their government.

A sharp chuckle escaped the web of Sarah's lips. "He lit the fire alright," it muttered as she dialed a familiar number. "Alex? You saw, right? Monroe dropped the bomb big, and vultures are circling like sharks."

Alex across town's eyes were red-rimmed from editing Monroe's speech. He answered, "They're more like hyenas, scavenging for scraps. But don't worry, Sarah, we'll be their hyena bait."

A low growl rumbled in Sarah's throat. "Good. We need to keep pressure on those snakes. Leak another file, something that's spicy, something that'll make their scales crawl."

"Consider it done. I got a juicy email chain here detailing Senator Harris' little soirée with Blackstone. The highest order of blackmail fodder." Alex's voice vibrated with the glee of a predator who had just gotten his claws on fresh meat.

Later, in the hushed refuge of Monroe's office, the mood was tense but tinged with hope. "They're scrambling, Senator," Sarah reported, tapping away at her keyboard. "The press hounds are on the scent, and their allies are wavering."

Monroe nodded, and a flicker of worry ran across his eyes. "Good, but don't become cocky. They're wounded, not dead. They'll come after us, and they'll aim for the jugular."

Alex, ever the pragmatist, chimed in, "We need to tighten our security, senator. They'll try to discredit you, leak dirt, or do anything to sway public opinion."

Monroe clenched his jaw. "They can try. But I won't back down. This isn't just about exposing their corruption. This is about restoring faith to our democracy."

That would be three of them; a trinity forged in the fire of righteous anger, huddled together, plotting their next move. The fight was far from over, but in the dim light of Monroe's office, a spark of hope flickered, a promise that the silent hunters would bring the wolves to heel.

The game afoot was played in whispers and shadows.

The once great Senate floor was reduced to the air turnings of wild scavengers, the thick scent of fear mixed with that of their own bloody hunger. And in the heart of it all, Monroe, the silent hunter, stalked his prey, waiting for the right moment to strike.

***

The silver fox named Senator Harris swirled the brandy in the crystal glass, the amber liquid capturing the glint of hidden cameras he believed lurked in the opulent corners. "Whispers, indeed," he drawled, his voice like aged Bourbon—smooth but potent. "But whispers can be as easily choked as they are breathed, wouldn't you agree, Senator Blackstone?"

Across the room, Senator Blackstone, a bulldog of a man with jowls that quivered with barely contained fury, slammed his fist down on the mahogany table. "Choked? We're not dealing with gossip rags here, Harris! This is a spy in our midst, someone who knows about our secrets."

"And pray tell, what do we propose to do about this spy?" Harris's voice was deceptively calm but held an edge of steel to it.

"Findin' it," Blackstone growled. "Flushin' it out. And when we do," He didn't need to finish the sentence; his meaning was plain, and the unspoken threat was heavy in the air.

One of the younger senators, Prescott, his face pale beneath a mop of sandy hair, piped up, "But how? We can't exactly announce to the world that we're holding clandestine meetings in a speakeasy beneath the Capitol."

Harris chuckled; dry and utterly devoid of amusement. "Prescott, my boy, discretion is our shield. We operate in the shadows, remember? And who needs an announcement when a little accident can do the trick?" His cold, calculating gaze met Blackstone's.

There was an understanding that passed between them, a grim pact that had been forged in the fires of fear and desperation. The unspoken promises crackled through the hot summer air, mingling with the veiled threats and leaving everyone uncomfortable and anxious around them.

The hunt was on, and blood mingled with the old ghosts of broken promises in the opulent halls of power, where deceit danced with ambition.

Chapter Six:
The Gathering Storm

Senator Monroe held the well-worn, leather-bound book in his hands; it was marked with the emblem of the Republic, imprinting his palm. The trio and their investigation were like miles away from the cold, fluorescent-lit room they inhabited. Sarah sat in a far corner of the living room, her hair pulled back into a bun, and as she furiously typed on the laptop, her face manifested a very concerned and concentrated look. Alex's eyes pinched over microfiche as he followed a finger across an image smudged by grain.

Alex managed, in a whisper, to wheeze out, "Senator, they know."

Monroe felt an icy shiver run down his backbone.

Sarah was not looking toward them as she added, "About us." Her fingers quivered a little, which exposed the fear that was eating her from the inside.

It was a moment of tension, broken by nothing but the muffled hum of the room's ventilation system and Sarah's annoying wristwatch, which ticked nervously. And the weight of their pursuit pressed them down from the burden of treading on holy, and therefore forbidden, territory.

"How?" Monroe asked me impatiently. There was no way that any one of them would betray each other.

Alex looked away, frowning as he muttered. "Unless there is a leak, An inside man."

The room's atmosphere started to reek of suspicion. They exchanged wary looks, each looking the other up and down for anomalies—a nervous twitch that would reveal any lingering, desperate fears. However, their countenances were neutral, like they had been trained in the art of disguise.

The book that was in Monroe's hand seemed to be heavier than ever before because the knowledge that it concealed had two sides. With every page that turned, they were exposed deeper, closer to the core of the conspiracy, but also closer to those who would do their best to hide and protect it all.

Suddenly, a rude knock on the door broke through the fragile silence. Their bodies stiffened; waves of adrenaline racing through their veins. Sarah slammed her laptop close; the screen was now like a mirror, reflecting their worried faces. Alex took the microfiche with trembling hands and stuffed it in his bag. Monroe's hand, in reflex, reached for the hidden gun tucked in the waistband of his trousers and said, "Who is it?"

There was no answer at first, only another persistent knock. After that came a muffled voice, harsh and gruff. "Police, open up!"

Monroe shared a desperate look with his fellow warriors. There was no escape. It clearly looked like a trap, and it probably trapped the trio within it.

Sarah clenched her jaw in frustration. Monroe's mind raced. The documents and the book could not end up in the wrong hands. He looked into Alex's eyes, and a silent moment passed between them without words.

More resigned than convinced, Monroe said, "Get rid of the obvious."

In a whirlwind of collective behavior, they shredded down the documents, they already have scanned, put all the encrypted files on a USB, and erased every digital footprint from their devices. The book and USB, however, were even more challenging. Its significance could not be easily dismissed. But time was running out. The pounding on the door became louder and louder, with the soft shuffling of feet and muffled conversations.

Monroe passed both of the things—the USB and the book—to Alex with a heavy heart. "Take it. Hide it somewhere safe. This cannot end with us."

Alex hesitated, his face etched with an understanding of the gravity of the situation. It was the burden of holding a secret that could destroy empires.

"I won't disappoint you, Uncle Monroe," he finally said, taking the book and USB and placing them in a secret compartment of his bag. It was the first time he addressed Monroe as an uncle.

As Alex climbed up the air ducts, there were tears in Monroe's eyes. Sarah rushed into the bathroom and turned on the shower, acting like she was about to take a shower.

Monroe pretended to make an attempt to tie his robe slowly as if he wanted to cover himself up since he knew it was too late for him to open the door.

Another knock came, and with that, the door crashed open, flooding the room with brutal light and grim figures in uniform. Their faces were blank, and their intentions were undefined. With his face set like a stoic mask, Monroe came forward into the open. "What the hell is happening, officers?"

The tension level was also high, with the outcome in a dangling state. The answer was going to define not only their destinies but also the future of the truth that they were trying to reveal. The line between justice and conspiracy had become indistinct, with both perched on the precipice of a chasm.

Alex looked down from the vent and saw the police officers coming closer to Monroe. Sarah looked at the scene going on from a slightly opened bathroom door.

Monroe's heart pounded against his rib cage, a frenetic accompaniment to the silence as it settled upon the room. The officers, two men in spotless uniforms, were stone-still, their faces devoid of expression. First, a young and fidgety one moved from foot to foot. The other, aged and stolid, looked at Monroe with eyes like chips of ice.

"Misunderstanding," the junior officer gasped finally, his voice guttural. "Wrong address about drug tip; you see, sometimes it happens."

Monroe arched an eyebrow, his eyes focused. "Drug tip? In a hotel room rented by a sitting senator?"

There was a clearing of the throat by the older officer, an irritating sound in this tense atmosphere. "Anonymous call, Senator; we had to come."

"And what were you planning to find exactly?" Monroe responded aggressively. "A stash of cocaine among my legislative proposals?"

The junior officer shifted and moved around the room, avoiding Monroe's gaze. The older officer showed no emotion; but the faintest hint of annoyance came through.

Monroe knew. The break-in, the practiced body movements, the subtle tensions in their gait—these weren't ordinary policemen. They were wolves in sheep's clothing, their uniforms a facade for their true purpose: silencing him forever.

"Senator," as the older officer spoke in a seemingly calm voice, expressed regret. "Sorry for any inconvenience. But you understand, duty calls."

"Duty or damage control?" Monroe retorted, his voice getting louder.

The youthful officer jerked, his hand pointing at the holster on his hip. The older officer gave him a warning glance, then turned back to Monroe with a predatory smile playing on his mouth.

"None, Senator," he drawled in a voice thick with mock sympathy. "We will go. Have a good night to you and Ms. Mitchell, sir."

Upon hearing Sarah's last name, Monroe realized that this was just the beginning of what they were going to face head-on.

***

Smoke from cigars filled the air, pungent and stifling, reproducing the ambiance of an illicit gathering. In the private room of a fancy D.C., restaurant, five shadowy figures gathered around a shining mahogany table. These were no ordinary diners; they were the "Shadow Five," a cabal of powerful politicians united by a dark secret and a singular purpose: to silence Monroe and his unrelenting investigation.

The wiry man with steel eyes, Senator Harris, tapped his slender fingers on the table and spoke in a low, rasping voice. "Gentlemen, this is intolerable. Monroe's investigation has revealed more than we expected. We need to act and move quickly."

Whispers of agreement hummed around the table. Senator Evelyn Mitchell, her features softened by a cloud of cigar smoke, spoke with clear distaste in her voice. "He is nothing but a fly that is stinging on an open sore. We cannot allow this man to reveal our meticulously made web."

Their faces, though hidden, were distorted in a collective grimace. Greed, ambition, and a fear of exposure weighed between them. The public faces they so carefully constructed hid the underlying system of graft that Monroe's relentless pursuit was threatening to lay bare.

The room froze before Senator Blackstone, whose harsh voice ripped the spell, "Termination. It's the only way out, but it has to be subtle, like a scalpel used by a surgeon."

As one unit, the group started to come up with ideas. Darker ideas bounced back and forth.

"Staging a car accident?" Senator Prescott recommended

"Poisoning," Harris himself added creepily. If a normal person was sitting between them, it would send chills down their spine.

However, Senator Evelyn, who was a woman notorious for her ruthlessness, had another proposal. "Victor Kinsley. He's the one. Our favorite Alchemist. His knowledge of undetectable toxins will make sure that everything is done quietly and with no trace left behind."

Their chosen instrument, Victor Kinsley, was a ghost in the shadows whose name was whispered with fear and respect. A man with a past darker than the poisons he made; his services were only sought by those who had secrets to hide.

The Shadow Five agreed, their voices low and cold, with hands holding a contract signed in the night. Victor Kinsley would be paid in full, a sum big enough to ensure his silence and cooperation. Monroe and his aides, Sarah and Alex, would be killed—only their deaths would be carefully staged as accidents, and the investigation into the truth would be gone with them.

***

Victor Kinsley, the latent dark figure in a white chef's apron, glided between canapés and cocktails with practiced grace in one of the events held by Senator Monroe. His smile was mischievous, and his words were beguiling, hiding the icy calculations that lurked just under the surface. His mission is to penetrate Senator Monroe's inner circle, win them over, and then silence them.

Sarah, Senator Monroe's alert assistant, had been chosen by him as his first target. Victor knew, his way with words. His charm was a magic spell that would work on any person at any time. Some believed that he had connections with the Illuminati, but then again, they were all stories at the end of the way.

"Has anyone ever told you that your eyes look like the exquisite combination of cardamom and dark chocolate?" Victor asked Sarah with a smile, "Myself, Victor."

Victor held out a hand for her.

"I'm Sarah, and no, Victor." Sarah gave her hand in his and said, "No, I haven't, but it sounds intriguing. Tell me more about it."

Victor leaned down and kissed her hand before letting it go. "I see. Well, the flavors intertwining is simply mesmerizing. It's an experience that ignites the senses, much like your presence here ignites my curiosity."

Sarah laughed at that comment. "I must admit that you have a way with words, and I must admit, your passion for food is quite captivating."

"Passion is a powerful force, isn't it?" Victor chuckled darkly. "Just like the passion I see in your eyes, when we discuss these delightful culinary adventures."

Sarah took a look around the room before she couldn't hold back as she said, "You certainly have a way of making even the simplest ingredients sound enchanting."

At that moment, Victor knew that his magic spell had been cast successfully. "Well, Sarah, the way I see it, life is too short for mediocre flavors and unremarkable experiences. Wouldn't you agree?"

"Absolutely." Sarah agreed with a nod of her head: "Mediocrity has no place in the kitchen, passion, or life."

Victor told stories of spice mixes and rare chocolates, and his eyes watched her reactions. He lightly mentioned unknown ingredients, seeing how her eyes sparkled with wonder and admiration.

But to Sarah's amazement, he had a real passion for food.

Their talk flowed. Victor tactfully piqued her interest while sowing seeds of trust. Senator Monroe called out for Sarah, and she excused herself from Victor.

The next target was easy. He saw Alex, the quiet and observant one, keeping an eye on everyone around him. At this point, Victor intercepted Alex while Sarah was being dragged toward another guest.

Looking at a faint symbol of a video game character on Alex's hoodie, Victor's eyes caught it and asked, "You wouldn't happen to be a gamer, would you?"

Alex's eyes darted in the direction of the symbol that was on his sleeve; there was a clash between surprise and disbelief in them. "Yeah. I dabble."

Victor smiled smugly, reaching for his phone. "In that case, you may well recognize this." Then he showed a screenshot of the regional gaming tournament leaderboard with the name "Phoenix-13" in front.

"No way!" Alex mumbled as he recognized his online alias.

Victor chuckled. "Isn't it a small world? I remember cheering you on during that epic comeback. Man, that was so cool!"

The ice was broken. At first, Alex was weary but got more and more involved in Victor's stories of the gaming industry.

The ice began cracking—cold and delicate. Alex was pulled almost willingly into Victor's game-world anecdotes. It was a common language, and Victor was an expert at manipulating it to bridge the gap between them inch by inch through shared jokes and inside references.

***

Victor gained presence in their lives, offering what seemed to be innocent assistance with chores and predicting what they required with his precision. As all this was happening, his ears were pricked, his mind listing every interchange, the details of their itineraries, and the manner of their movements.

Finally, the time presented itself—a weekend jaunt organized by the senator and his staff. The ideal opportunity for relaxation and manipulation. Victor offered his catering services, his offer oozing enthusiasm and flavorful delights.

Victor's charm and thoroughness persuaded Sarah, who at first was reluctant. Alex, on the other hand, was still a thorn in his flesh, with his eyes wondering 'what if' situations everywhere. Victor knew that he had to take things slowly, earn their full trust, and then end them with his deadly plan.

"Think of it as a culinary adventure," Victor insisted, his voice warm. "Picture yourself starting your day with the fragrance of fresh croissants, savoring local delicacies made with true dedication."

There appeared to be a spark of interest in Sarah's eyes. "Locally sourced, you say?"

That's exactly what Victor was waiting for. He nodded, his smile widening. "Yes. Think about tasting the freshest catch from the nearby lake coupled with vegetables grown on a farm by yours truly."

The bait was set. The trap, disguised as a lush paradise, lay ready to be sprung. However, would the prey see through the disguise, or would they fall for the illusion? Like an enigmatic hidden ingredient in Victor's dishes, the answer stayed enshrouded in suspense.

***

The anticipation crackled in the crisp mountain air, when Senator Monroe, Sarah, and Alex arrived at the cabin. Surrounded by towering pines, the cozy lodge offered a refuge from the stress of their investigation. However, beneath the superficial picture of harmony, the invisible net of hypocrisy waited.

Monroe looked around alertly and had a feeling of uneasiness in his stomach when he looked into the woods. "It's too quiet," he murmured, getting out of the car.

Without any regard for his worry, Sarah was busy snapping pictures of beautiful scenery. "Fresh air and some rest from all those stuffy committee rooms—just what we needed," she chirped.

Alex, known to be quiet, never responded, his eyes resting on the tree-line. Not even his casual appearance could hide the worry that lurked beneath his placid façade.

Unbeknownst to them; their arrival was carefully monitored. Miles away, in a dimmed room full of electronic equipment, the Shadow Five and their security team followed their every step.

Victor, his face set, straightened his earpiece. "Visual verification. The target has arrived at the destination point."

On a screen monitored by a hooded figure called Wraith, he adjusted a satellite feed. "Surveillance drones are connected to the Internet. Encrypted audio and video feed."

Senator Evelyn leaned forward in her chair with steely eyes. "Remember, Wraith. There is no room for error. This operation must be flawless. Elimination is our only priority."

Wraith's voice remained emotionless. "I understand. The protocol calls for minimal intervention. My operatives will be out of sight like the shadows watching the shadows."

The idyllic scene the trio saw at the cabin over the miles mocked their enemies' evil plans. Monroe, relaxing by the fireplace, couldn't get rid of the feeling of being watched. He saw the fleeting movement outside in the woods, but when he went to have a look, he found nothing.

Sarah, absorbed in scrutinizing the new facts, treated his worries as exhaustion. "Senator. Chill out, enjoy the scenery."

But Alex noticed the doubt in Monroe's eyes. He pulled him aside, his voice low. "Something feels off. Did you see?"

"Ssshhhh…" Sarah moved forward and put a finger on Alex's lips. "Nothing is happening. I know it is a boring place, but please chill out both of you."

Alex retorted, "Yeah. I am fully relaxed because your philosophical lover is not here to annoy us."

"You did not say that!" Sarah grabbed a pillow from the couch and started to hit Alex, to which Monroe couldn't help but smile as he relaxed in his chair.

"Wait, let me take that back." Alex stopped Sarah.

"Good boy." Sarah smiled.

"Victor ain't a lover boy. He is a blind boy." Alex said as he stood up, "Because, he clearly couldn't see your red flags, Sarah."

With that, Alex sprinted outside, and Sarah ran after him. Senator Monroe looked at them from the window and saw them getting engaged in a snowball fight.

That's exactly what he wanted for Sarah and Alex.

For Alex, he wanted a peaceful life, and far away from the world of politics, as his best friend and fellow senator would have wanted.

On the other hand, Sarah may be older than Alex, but she neglected her inner child for so long, and now that Victor is in her life, Senator Monroe couldn't help but be grateful.

Before their departure for this winter getaway, Victor asked for Senator Monroe's blessing to marry Sarah. He promised the senator that he would propose to her the very next day after dinner. It would double the fun of the vacation.

***

Victor arrived later that day, as Monroe, Sarah, and Alex were living under an invisible net. Small, evil-minded spider-sized cameras masquerading as harmless things were attached to their rooms and vehicles; their lenses transmitted a steady flow of information to the invisible observers in the dark. Like puppeteers pulling invisible strings, the Shadow Five knew their every move and their every plan.

As the evening settled on Saturday, the cabin became shrouded in a false peace, the air heavy with the aroma of burning wood and a promise of tranquility. Safe on the inside, the three sat before the warm, crackling fireplace, unaware of the predator preparing to attack from within.

Victor Kinsley, disguised as a wolf in sheep's clothes, was already inside the cabin, apparently playing the role of a caring caretaker. With practiced ease, he had arranged a feast, each dish filled with a slow-acting poison made to simulate the creeping chill of hypothermia, the last scene of a play.

"Dinner is served," Victor called out to everyone as he set the table.

Sarah walked up to him first and kissed his cheek. "This looks delicious."

Victor smiled and said, "Thank you. Eat it before it gets cold or worse, it turns you cold." He joked, making Sarah laugh. Nobody knew about Victor's motives and agendas.

Gradually, as they explored the mouthwatering aromas and tastes, a shift occurred inside them. Bizarre fatigue settled in Monroe's limbs, and a creeping sensation of growing coldness pricked at Sarah's skin. Alex, ever watchful, detected the trembling in their hands and the shade growing on their faces. His stomach did not just churn because of the delicious meal; the meal stirred up an uneasiness in his stomach.

Alex inquired, "Are you feeling okay, Senator?" His tone reflected his facial expressions, which were full of worry.

Victor, his eyes cold and gleaming with satisfaction, watched from the darkness. The poison was doing its work, spreading its coldness inside its unsuspecting victims. In time, they would be devoured, their deaths declared a tragic accident, and their search for the truth would go to the grave with them.

Chapter Seven:
Beneath The Veil Of Lies

"Something's wrong," Sarah croaked; her voice broke as she spoke. The walls of the room seemed to tilt, and the edges of her peripheral vision were blurring; everything swam before her eyes. Her arms and legs felt heavy and weighted, pulling her down towards the floor. Panic clawed at her throat, but she couldn't even scream.

Alex, however, slumped to the wall by her side, his stricken face melting away into one of terror. "Ca-can't breathe," he coughed each word.

Senator Monroe, usually the embodiment of stoicism, was now clutching his chest while coldness spread into his veins. "Poisoned," he gasped, his voice hardly more than a whisper. "Victor."

The name hung heavy, out in the air with accusations and dread. In icy certainty, they knew that the trusted chef was a traitor now.

Fear and helplessness coiled around them; squeezing the air from their lungs.

A creak in the shadows made Sarah's spine tingle, and Victor stepped out with his predatory smile gleaming with chilly satisfaction, lighting up his eyes. "Such a pity," he purred, his smooth voice like silk laced with venom. "The truth dies with you."

Sarah felt a surge of defiance. She could not let him just get away with it. "You won't get away with this," she hissed, hardly audible.

Victor chuckled—a cruel, hollow sound. "Oh, that I have. Your deaths will be considered accidents—another bad twist of fate. By the time anyone suspects, I'll be miles away enjoying the fruits of my labor."

Her gaze caught with Alex's before flicking to the Senator's; it was desperation in the same amount of determination. They wouldn't give in—not now. They had to find a way, any-way, to expose Victor and survive.

"We have to... We have to warn someone," the senator croaked, almost in a whisper. "Someone, who can trust us..."

But the dizziness cut off what he was saying. His eyes fluttered closed, his breath rising and falling in short, labored waves.

"Senator!" Sarah screamed as she reached out, but her hand only met empty air. Panic sparked, cold and pervasive. If the senator falls, who will ever believe them? Who would fight for them once their voices were forever lost?

Her eyes frantically roved the room, looking for anything at all that would be of help. Finally, her eyes fell on a heavy brass lamp on a side table. With a sudden surge of adrenaline, she lunged for it and snatched it up with the last of her strength.

"Back off," she said, showing the lamp as if it were a sword. Victor's smile wavered, and his features rolled in surprised expressions. He hadn't expected such desperation and defiance from a dying woman.

All or nothing now. He flinched, and at that moment, Sarah moved in with all her strength and aimed at the side of his head.

Sarah's lunge came weak, the lamp shaking in her weakened grasp. Victor was surprised for just a second, and then, the predatory smile returned. But before he could react any further, the tension in the room broke with a high-pitched and bloodcurdling scream. It wasn't Sarah's scream; it was Alex's, with his eyes coming out like rubber balls, gripping his throat and taking deep breaths.

Panic clutched the woman's heart in an icy grip. The realization that Victor had planned for resistance jolted her with horror. Planted somewhere, perhaps far from here and not yet heard, was a sophisticated radio jammer that would cut them off from the outside world. Their cries for help would just echo in the silence, witnesses to their struggle being only the cold and uncaring walls.

That isolation pressed on them, a suffocating shroud. Victor's words, the chilling poison, their torturous situation—the three together united, holding no hope other than oppressive despair. The air felt heavy with each labored breath, and as it blurred their vision further with each flicker of fatigue, darkness threatened to swallow them whole.

And, from that desperation, burned a glimmer of defiance that refused to succumb. Sarah would not yield until there was no spark of life left in her. She took a glance at the senator, his back hunched against the wall, his face contorted in agony, and at that moment, she saw the steely glint in his eyes. This fight was theirs, even if their voices were stolen and their cries went unheard.

With an outburst of an adrenaline rush that belied her weakening body, she threw the lamp towards the nearest window. The glass shattered onto the floor, its sound echoing against the imposed silence. She ignored the sharp sting of flying glass shards and hurried toward the opening, gasping for the cool night air that seemed to hold out a snippet of hope for her.

But Victor had already seen this coming. He lunged, his cold hand snatching around her wrist, his voice a hiss of venom. "Nowhere to run, little bird. Your song ends here."

Sarah fought her pure primal urge for life, fueling her. With the last of her strength, she jammed her heel down onto his foot and he yelled with pain. In that second of distraction, she wrenched her arm free and tumbled through the broken window to land hard on the cold stone patio below.

Pain shot through her ankle, but she ignored it and scrambled to her feet. The night air whipped in her face, bringing some distant sounds of the city—an unwilling reminder of help so close and yet so far. Victor's bellow of rage echoed behind her, spurring her forward.

But her attempt to escape was short-lived. Her fragile body, consumed by poison, had betrayed her. Her lungs were on ice, her legs throbbed, and the world spiraled with her. Then, just as Victor's thundering steps were on the brink of reaching her, the darkness swallowed her, pulling her into a frigid chasm.

Victor then, took Sarah in his arms and went back to the cabin, where Alex and Senator Monroe were almost losing the battle of their lives.

The inside of the cabin was cooling around them; a warm shroud of death surrounded them. A vague light of awareness flickered, an ember going out amidst the overwhelming darkness. The poison had further laced its icy grip, turning their limbs into leaden weight. Each shallow breath rasped in their throats, a testament to their failing battle.

Senator Monroe's face twisted in pain and grim realization. "Sarah, Alex," he rasped, propped against the wall, his voice coming out like a hoarse whisper, barely escaping the tremble of his lips. "My k-kids..." The words hung in the air like the plummeting temperature, a congealing confirmation of their planned demise set in motion. He knew with cold certainty that the end was approaching and their fight was over.

There was silence, only the tortured gasps of the battle for life in the depths of the night. Victor also messed up with the circuit breakers in the cabin as the lights went out, making their deaths look more believable.

Senator Monroe, Alex, and Sarah had been puppets in the hands of a sick play, with strings pulled by an invisible hand and their voices devoured in the silent chokehold of the radio jammer.

Dawn came, tinged with orange and pink—an inverse of the cruelty of the night.

A group of young hikers with a desire for adventure discovered the secluded cabin in the quiet wilderness. The view that appeared at them could freeze any innocent heart. There lay three figures, spread out and lifeless; the trace of a tragedy was imprinted on their faces.

The hikers stepped in out of fear and morbid curiosity. One of them carefully swung open the creaking door, and the pervading stench of death welcomed them. What had happened became obvious; curiosity turned into panic.

By the time law enforcement and emergency services arrived, there was nothing to be done. It was a perfectly believable pronouncement. Death by hypothermia and exposure. The frigid temperatures, the storm that had raged through the previous night, and the isolated serenity of the cabin—a perfectly tragic accident.

Their bodies were carried away, and the cabin stood silent again, its secrets buried under the blanket of new snow.

***

Washington, D.C., draped itself in mourning: the flags at half-mast, the solemn pronouncements filling the air, the somber procession making its way through the streets, ending with the late Senator Monroe, his personal assistant Sarah Mitchell, and his godson Alex Turner lying in state beneath the soaring rotunda. The city grieved for the man they were so fond of.

But in the grandstands of national grieving, another story was being played. Below, in the dim light of the chambers of the Capitol, where shadows stretched long and secrets clung to the air, a group of senators celebrated. Words of "mission accomplished" and "finally out of the picture" passed among them. Senator Monroe, the thorn in the side, the champion of transparency and accountability, was silenced.

Senator Harris had glared down at the gathering with sharp features in an exaggerated, predatory grin. "His death presented an opportunity we couldn't afford to miss. The void he leaves. We will fill it."

"But who?" said Senator Blackstone, his eyes gleaming with ambition as he leaned forward.

"A puppet, of course," Senator Harris laughed, his voice cold and calculating. "Easily manipulated, someone loyal to our cause."

Their eyes came to rest on a portrait that was hanging on the wall—Senator Prescott, our young and ambitious senator, but a man of the most impressionable nature and a person of flexible character.

"He's perfect," whispered Senator Evelyn, curling her lips in a smirk with satisfaction.

The whole room hummed in unison. The game was on: use their influence, control the media, and engineer a campaign to paint Prescott as the successor, the one to carry on as the hope of the grieving nation. He would be their puppet, a facade hiding their latent agendas.

But their celebration was broken by the sound of a knock on the door. An assistant with a very pale face peeked in rather nervously. "The press. They're asking about the senator's death. His toxicology report. It came back inconclusive."

Hushed exclamations exploded throughout the room. "Inconclusive?" Senator Harris snarled, a frown muscling up into his features like a snuffed candle. "It couldn't be; we were so careful."

"Somebody's digging," murmured Senator Blackstone, squinting his eyes. "We need to act quickly. Silence them, control the leaks, and control the narrative, before it spirals out of control."

An awkward hush fell over the whole room, the grim sense of reality now pushing hard on their conscience. Their carefully planned coup, their coronation—all of it was on the brink of disaster.

The death of Senator Monroe was meant to secure their hold, but it could be the one thing that undid everything they had built.

"Plant another story," retorted Senator Harris, his eyes sparking with cold calculation. "An anonymous source, a leaked document— anything to cast doubt on the investigation and solidify our version of events."

The aide quickly replied, "The reporter's digging deeper into Monroe's finances. She suspects suspicious activity surrounding some recent contracts."

A collective groan hummed through the room. The reporter, on the other hand, was notorious for being tenacious with investigative matters.

"Silence her and Victor," Senator Evelyn hissed, her voice full of venom. "But discreetly. No more messy accidents like Monroe's."

On the other hand, Senator Prescott, their scrupulously chosen tool, bathed in the glow of the limelight. The secret cabal of lawmakers won; their web of deception stretched like cancer through the very heart of Washington.

Senator Harris, the architect of this scheme, stood in the room talking to his cohorts. "Prescott does well," he said, with a sardonic note in his voice. "The public mourns Monroe, and he embodies the perfect image of stability and continuity."

Senator Blackstone leaned back in his chair. "Still, whispers persist," he added, "with rumors of the senator's sudden demise. We need to snuff them before they take root."

Senator Evelyn smiled evilly before saying, "Oh, we will."

Chapter Eight:
A Chance Encounter

Amid all the busy streets of Washington, D.C., Brett was moving around as a local, not just as a visitor but still as an undercover agent on a secret mission. Out of work, he took this as his chance to blend in with the locals, scouring the streets for clues and new hideouts where the city's dark side gorged and hatched plans.

The D.C. city, full of history, was made up of a lot of secrets that Brett didn't even know about. While wandering the glittering streets, the autumn leaves golden color seemed to reveal the unsolved riddles, and the crisp air held the implication of peril hiding in the darkness.

Amid a crowd of people, Brett, a man from California's sunny coast, disguised his true identity with practiced ease. His job took him to the very center of the nation's capital, where power and ambition would clash in a fatal waltz. Brett understood all too well that his D.C. stay was temporary, but the importance of the assignment made the passing of time feel like an eternity.

While, he was diving into the city's covert network, Brett found an intricate web of corruption and fraud, which was disguised to drown everything dear to him. At each restaurant he ate, and at each site he visited, the risk of danger and revelation was possible. The historical landmarks of the city were so charming that they easily concealed the evil deeds that were going on in the locked rooms under them.

In D.C., nights, the tension was building up as Brett stepped carefully, knowing that every step could lead to a breakthrough or a fatal trap. The spell of the city was irresistible, and it entangled him in the intrigue that was testing his determination and his devotion to the cause.

As time passed by, Brett's resolve to uncover the truth only intensified, pulling him into a world of high-class espionage and pulse-pounding suspense.

His experience in the capital city came to be a battle against time as he strived to reveal the dark forces that wanted to tear the fabric of the nation apart.

In the capital city, where power and ambition dominated the system, Brett's life in California seemed to be an ancient history, overpowered by the adrenaline-pumping reality of his mission in Washington, D.C.

Brett walked down the lively streets of Washington, D.C., with a subtle feeling of tension in the air. The inviting café called out to him, promising a temporary refuge from the bitter cold outside. The fragrance of freshly brewed coffee subtly blended with the warmth of the coffee shop interior, painted a picture of coziness against the backdrop of the tension surrounding his task.

Brett ordered a latte and went near the window to sit down. His mind was occupied with the secret meeting he was about to attend tomorrow. He had no idea that the universe was actually playing matchmaker on that very day.

Brett was unaware that Emma Hayes, a bright and breathtakingly beautiful journalist, was sitting at the table beside him and scribbling some notes on the yellow legal pad. She had a reputation for being a straight-shooter in Washington, D.C., and no other power player could compare to her influence in the city's inner circles.

Despite the fact that Emma's unshakable spirit of justice would many times bring her into conflict with the very men that she was trying to expose, she remained resolute. The fact that she wanted to achieve greatness in her career was manifested through her attention to detail in her work, and she would often get absorbed in the world of journalism and forget about the threats that were around.

COFFEE
BAR

With their minds occupied by their own thoughts, Brett and Emma settled down. The barista, a young woman with an aura of mystery around her, moved between the tables, her eyes revealing a knowledge of the city's secrets.

"Here you go, sir," the barista said, her eyes fixed on Brett just a little more than they should be. "Appreciating the city, huh?"

Brett nodded and smiled in return. "Yes, it is quite different compared to back home, but I am getting used to it."

However, Emma's deep concentration was broken when the barista came to her table. "Another round of black coffee, Miss Hayes?" The barista's voice had an undercurrent of concern and a shared understanding of the dangers that lurked in the city.

Emma lifted her gaze to see the barista looking at her. "Yes, please. Thank you," she said with a note of urgency in her voice that only a fellow truth seeker would understand.

As the barista moved away from the tables and to the counter, Brett and Emma both of them, carried their own secrets and agendas in the labyrinthine streets of Washington, DC. Nevertheless, they did not know that their fates were destined to cross, entangled in a web of intrigue, and danger, which would draw them into the game of lies and uncovering.

Emma's eyes glinted as she glanced at the open pages that lay before her while sipping her cappuccino. A soft hum of the conversation pervaded the room; amid the quiet noise, her eyes noticed Brett, who was lost in his thoughts, his laptop illuminating his face. He had a special aura around him, a magnetic force that was attracting her and stirring something deep inside her that she was not able to comprehend.

Brett felt her eyes on him, his movements becoming more animated as his hand accidentally tipped the empty cup of coffee over, attracting the attention of the other patrons of the cafe. There was a soft chuckle that escaped from Emma's lips, and she moved to his side while watching the scene unfold.

"You seem to be having a tough day," she remarked, a friendly smile gracing her lips as she approached him.

Brett's cheeks flushed with embarrassment as he fumbled for words. "Uh, yeah, I guess, I was a bit lost in my thoughts."

Unspoken curiosity danced in Emma's eyes as she studied him. "I couldn't help but notice you seem a bit out of place here. Are you new to D.C.?"

Brett's laughter filled the air, finding her charm disarming. "Yeah, just here on business. I'm from California."

Emma extended her hand, introducing herself. "Emma Hayes, journalist. It's a pleasure to meet you."

Brett shook her hand with a warm smile. "Brett Evans, consultant. Likewise, Emma."

The discussion seemed to proceed by itself, each moment bringing them closer together into a net of common interests and unspoken emotions. Brett was mesmerized by Emma's intelligence and grace, and he became eager to unravel the mystery of her knowledge about the city.

During their conversations, Emma's knowledge about D.C.'s dark side caught Brett's attention and made him want to learn more. Their professional lives merged into one as they swapped tales and thoughts.

Emma leaned in, her eyes alight with a mixture of curiosity and a hint of mischief. "You know, Brett, D.C., is more than what meets the eye. Below the shiny surfaces of power and politics, there's a dark side; a side that very few dare to probe into."

Brett was intrigued as he looked at Emma, who was striking a mysterious pose. "My entire life, I've been curious about digging up the truth, no matter how deep it is buried. Spill it out, Emma. What is the city's secret?"

Emma reclined, a conspiratorial grin curling at the corners of her mouth. "Oh, Brett, the stories, I can tell you. The halls of power are not only places for ambition and influence but also treachery and lies. In this world, alliances are often short-lived and are regularly tested, and people sometimes have to pay the price."

Brett's mind buzzed with ideas; the adrenaline rush of finding out the mysteries of the city fed the flame that was burning inside him. "I didn't comprehend that Washington, D.C., was so interesting. You certainly have opened my eyes to a side of this city that I never knew existed."

As the conversation continued, they did not know that their encounter in the cafe had triggered a series of events that took their destinies and combined them in a way that they could not have imagined. The streets of the city shared its shadows with them and hinted at hidden hazards and unimaginable secrets, and the more Brett and Emma were drawn to that world of suspense and intrigue, the more they were afraid to push the limits of their desires and put their courage to the test.

The more Brett worked in Washington, DC, the more he struggled to forget about Emma, the mysterious girl he had met at the café. There was something about her that didn't leave his mind—a link that kept pulling his thoughts even when he was exploring the city's dark side.

After a few days of thinking, Brett was back at the coffee shop, where he had met Emma for the first time. He could not believe his eyes when he saw that she was sitting at a corner table with a book in her hand. As he neared her, a shy smile appeared on her lips, and they soon plunged into a conversation again. Their conversation flowed without any problems, and at the end, they swapped phone numbers, hoping, though secretly, to meet once again.

In the days after, Brett and Emma found themselves in a net of late-night discussions and connections. They talked about their feelings, hopes, and fears. All this made them feel safe; as they were together during the turmoil in their lives. With Emma at the center of his world, Brett found his feet in the darkness, a safe place to rest during the storm.

On one particular day, as Brett and Nexus were engaged in an important meeting, his phone suddenly pinged with a message from Emma. A blush covered his face as he mumbled an apology, realizing that he had disrupted the meeting. Agent Smith gave him a scornful look, asking him to concentrate on the present matter.

"Sorry, it is just a quick message," Brett mumbled, his fingers tapping out a rapid response to Emma. He couldn't help but steal a quick look at her profile picture and smile as he caught himself blushing as he returned to her work.

Agent Smith cleared his throat, and Brett found his attention drawn to the meeting. "Brett, we need your full attention here," he reprimanded; a trace of irritation in his voice.

"Of course, Smith," Brett said, dragging his eyes away from his phone. Despite his attempts to concentrate, his mind kept evading back to the words he had told her—the feeling of connectedness that crossed over their boundaries and unified their distant worlds.

As the meeting went on, Brett found himself pulled between duty and passion. The weight of his professional commitments, though, seemed to squeeze him while his heart was longing for something more with Emma. The town's secrets and the intoxicating nature of forbidden relationships had woven together to create a fascinating game of suspense and yearning, and Brett was caught in its web, unable to escape the grip of destiny.

Chapter Nine:
Bond Deepens And Crossroads

The rain was lashing the rooftop bar, and the neon cityscape had turned impressionist. Brett moved a little closer to the flickering candles, his glass of scotch causing the shadows on his face to dance. Then his phone buzzed once, and one sentence appeared on the glass screen: "Meet me at the Raven's Perch tonight. Come alone."

No name, no explanation. Just a dare from a ghost. He hesitated a moment, then texted back, "Who is this?"

He got a message in response almost immediately: "You know who. The answer's waiting."

He stared at the message. The rain drummed an implacable rhythm on the glass roof. Curiosity, in his life, was like the most dangerous drug. He downed his scotch and went to the Raven's Perch.

As soon as he got there, he found Emma sitting on the bar stool, looking at the city's lights.

11:28 AM
57%
Messages
UNKNOWN
Contact
Meet me at the
Raven's Perch tonight.
Come alone.
iMessage
Send

"Brett," she said, her voice a husky whisper, "you came."

He leaned in closer, keeping his voice low. "What's with the air of mystery? Why the Raven's Perch? Why the games? You changed your number?"

She cocked her head, the smile somehow now laced with a mischievous edge. "Because sometimes, shadows offer the best light and, yeah, a new number."

"Shadows," he repeated, the word like a mouthful of ash. "What are you hiding, Emma?"

She met his gaze, his eyes a storm brewing. "The truth. And maybe a way to lure you into my trap."

He laughed at her attempt to be mysterious, but there was a hint of a tremor in his voice. "We both know there's no way out of your traps."

Emma smiles as she realizes that Brett caught on. "There's always a way, Brett. It only comes with a price. A choice that you'll have to make. Over your feelings." She flirted

The city lights seemed to stagger in the rain-streaked windows, taking on aesthetic forms as if mimicking the conversation going on. The air seemed to hum with unspoken affection, with the promise of mystery just under the tenor of their talk.

"What choice?" He said, his hand having naturally gone for Emma's shoulder.

Emma leaned closer, her lips brushing his ear. "Who are you working for, Brett? And how far are you willing to go to keep your secrets?"

Those words hung in the air, a solitary shot in the silence. The rain roared outside to provide a fitting soundtrack to the storm that was brewing inside of him. Brett looked at Emma into her eyes to find some answers, some truth that would lead them out of this dangerous conversation Emma was dragging him into.

"I work for Emma; she is a beautiful woman and a brilliant journalist who sucks at being mysterious." Brett chuckled.

Emma let out a laugh. "You got me, Evans."

They both laughed together and talked about the weather and current affairs, melting the ice between them. But for a while, this was not a roof rendezvous but a dance on the tightrope with city lights sparkling behind Brett like a backdrop to the deadliest secret waiting to be revealed.

And so, on that very night, enrobed in the smoky embrace of such a cozy, laidback speakeasy, conversation moseyed its way into the arena of Brett's work.

In a voice threaded with worry, Emma asked, "So, really, Brett, what is it? What brings you here, in the down-low, anyway?"

He hesitated, like pebbles caught in his throat. "It's... it's kind of complicated, Emma. Let's just say, I'm here to right a wrong."

Her gaze sharpened. "A wrong? What kind of wrong?"

He met her eyes, the truth a bitter pill on his tongue. "There was a mission back in Prague. Things went south. People got hurt. And I owe it to them and to myself to set things right."

Emma leaned closer, her breath warm against his ear. "Who got hurt, Brett? And who do you owe this debt to?"

Every word was a thread pulling at his carefully woven lie, and his heart banged like a bird trapped against the walls of his ribcage, her scrutiny heavy upon his shoulders. "I can't tell you everything, Emma," he strained. "It's too dangerous."

But truth had a way of spilling through cracks, and he saw the first flicker of suspicion—the dawning awareness that maybe the man she was falling for wore a mantle of shadows. "For whom, Brett?" she rumbled low. "For you or for me?"

Silence hung in the air like a chasm was opening between them. Where once it was a safe place for whispered secrets, it is now a prison, and the music it played seemed mocking with unspoken fears they shared.

The night ended with more questions, and the chilling uncertainty that served as the city lights behind the foreground of their growing romance, now seemed to mirror the storm they battled within their hearts, which threatened to wash them away—as the secrets Brett did everything to keep buried.

***

On a Saturday evening, Brett rejected Emma's feelings for him. The bistro lights blurred in tears that came to Emma's eyes, reflecting in the ruby red of her unfinished wine. "Protecting my heart, Brett? Or protecting yourself from getting too close?"

His gaze darted, and the accusation was keen and cutting. The warmth seemed to leach from the bistro, replaced by a suffocating chill. "You know that's not true, Emma."

"Do I?" she countered, her voice cracking. "Every time I get closer; you push me away. You dangle intimacy like a carrot, then retreat back into the shadows."

He clenched his jaw. Her words were true and a bitter pill to swallow. "My job, Emma. It's dangerous. I can't drag you into that mess."

"But you already have, Brett," she whispered, her voice barely above a sob. "You've dragged me into your heart, and now you're building walls around it."

Silence pressed on the walls around, dense and suffocating; it muffled the other patrons to whispered conversations; their own drama boomed in the space.

"There's another reason, isn't there?" She probed fear and defiance fighting in her voice. "Something, you've left out."

He hesitated. There was more, and the burden of this secret would kill him. "There are things, I am not going to tell you, Emma. Things that are best left for anyone to not know about me."

"And me?!" she finally exclaimed, her voice losing its pitch in her frustration. "Don't I deserve to know the truth? Don't I deserve a chance to choose whether your secrets are worth the risk?"

His eyes were full of a storm of emotions. He saw the pain, the fear, and the glint of love that never died.

"I—" He began in a surprisingly hoarse voice. But he did not have the time to finish, as all of a sudden, a commotion rose at the entrance.

A tall figure lurking in the shadow looked over the room and fixed a lock-on stare on Brett. And in that moment, the air sizzled with tension, and this homely bistro had turned into a battlefield.

"Brett," Emma hissed loudly, trying to sound grave. "Who is that?"

It was Agent Smith, but Brett lied to him, saying that he was sleeping in the safe house in order to go out on a secret date with Emma.

Brett had a grip on Emma's hand. "We need to get out of here."

Without any reply from Emma, he started to take her with him towards the back exit, and thus, their escape was a desperate scramble ahead of the storm. Truth, lost in the darkness, transformed into a beast and was now running away from them. Their meager love story was about to collide with a dangerous reality.

As soon as Emma turned around to ask Brett about it, He just walked away, ignoring her.

***

On Valentine's Day, Emma was ready to brace herself and her love for Brett. It had been months, since she first met Brett. The spark that first flamed was now a steady, unyielding inferno. But Brett—the man who she fell for—remained a stranger. He spoke very generally about his work as a "consultant," coming and going out of town, whose calendar was secret. Tonight, there was no shaking of the insistent suspicion.

"Brett," she said, the words only a flutter above the clinking of glasses, "we haven't really been that honest with each other, have we?"

Brett paused with his fork still half-raised from his plate, something flickering over his face—a shadow of doubt that crept outside the man who always wore a cool mask. "What do you mean, Emma?"

"You never talk about your life in California," she said, looking steadily at him. "Or the company where you work—what really brings you to DC every few weeks? To be honest, it really starts sounding like a web of deceit."

Brett said nothing in reply, and his silence seemed to bear heavily on the room, almost physically palpable. It was only a matter of time before this moment would come; the truth had been a ticking time bomb between them for so long now, poised to ruin the delicate link. He took in another huge breath and locked eyes with her.

"There's a reason that I haven't been more honest with you, Emma," he stated, the words strained and so quiet. "There's a reason that's so much more than business. What I'm about to tell you is that it's got to stay in this room. You've got to promise me that."

Emma leaned forward, her apprehension locked in battle with her curiosity. "I promise, Brett. I won't ever repeat whatever it is."

He just let the floodgates open—a monsoon of secrets that had been held back for so long. There was a secret operation, stolen government documents, and top officials on either side of the fence.

As he talked, sentence by sentence, a chill raced up Emma's back, and the journalist in her was full of fear and excitement.

"So, you're an undercover agent?" She whispered after a while, her voice barely louder than her breath.

"Not exactly," Brett corrected her. "More like the private sector, off the record. This is bigger than the FBI, deeper than they can imagine."

He revealed the pieces of the mission, all those enigmatic clues that had haunted him so far, the shadowy figures that pulled the strings from such a distance. And as he told everything, Emma saw the man differently: not suave and charming, not the one she loved, but a guy toughened up from the game, living on the edge of life.

"And you think I can help?" She asked, and a sparkle of something glowed in her eyes, which could not at all be called different from resolute.

"You probably could," said Brett. "I mean, your connections, access to the information... It could be a great help. But it's dangerous, Emma. I don't want to put you at risk."

A mischievous smile curled her lips. "Don't underestimate me, Brett. I've been navigating the underbelly of Washington, D.C., for years. Maybe together, we have a shot at this web of deceit."

For a moment, their eyes locked, and in the darkness, a pact was sealed by the unspoken promise. The light of the candle flickered, casting gruesome shadows on the walls, reminding one of the dangers that lurked outside. They were no longer lovers having a shared meal but had become partners who found themselves playing a game, dangerous to death, in which their love story was attached to a struggling adventure for truth and justice. The stage was set, the curtain went up, and the play was about to begin.

***

As days bled into weeks, Emma and Brett's each meeting was like a clandestine operation in some dimly lit café or anonymous park. Emma, the daring reporter, would negotiate the murky contacts, wrangling some favor from someone and information from whispers of the stolen documents with the other.

Brett, the mysterious operative, leads her deeper into the maze; linking up the chains of cryptic messages and shadowy figures. And the bond between them, girded by shared danger and a pump of adrenaline, grew stronger with each passing day.

"This is crazy, Brett," Emma finally burst out after another one of those tension-packed meetings with a nervous, fidgety informant. "We're chasing ghosts, playing a game with people who hold way more power than we can even fathom."

Brett leaned in closer, the setting sun shadowing his eyes. "We're not just chasing ghosts, Emma. We're here for the truth, and the truth has a way of biting us back. Remember why we're doing this? For the lives that are at stake and for the secrets that could bring this city down."

Emma nodded at that, the frightful glint leaving her eyes, only to be replaced by a steely hardness. "You're right. We can't back off now. We've never been closer to catching them; I can feel it."

And those long nights had meant more than simply strategy between them and documents. Stolen moments under the moonlight and fueled by stolen kisses, along with whispered promises—

vulnerabilities on both parts totally unexpected yet evident even in their intimacy.

One night, in a backroom bar, huddled against the cold, a grizzled reporter slid a worn envelope across the table.

"This," he rasped, "is what you've been looking for. But be warned, kid. Knowledge is a heavy burden."

Emma tore open the envelope; her heart banged against her ribs. Classified documents, names redacted, pointed to an insinuation of conspiracy all the way through to the top power echelons.

She felt a cold sweat down her spine. "This is bigger than we thought," she breathed, her voice unsteady. "We've got to get this out, expose them before they do something to stop us."

The look in Brett's eyes took on a steely glint. "That is our endgame, Emma. But first, we need to know their game and their weaknesses. We've got to play them; get close enough to make the kill."

A thrilling dance with death was a dangerous proposition. Yet, in Emma's and Brett's lives, the line of distinction between love and duty had been muddled. They were now in a partnership in crime, and their hearts were tangled with a mission that could wrench them away or bind them forever.

***

The grainy video, downloaded from an anonymous source, flickered on Brett's laptop screen, casting the recording with an eerie green hue, highlighting the cramped apartment it was shot in. It recorded how a suspicious, hooded shadow was nervously making its way into the dark, abandoned alleyway.

Emma leaned in closer, and her breath escaped her as she said, "This is it, Brett. This is the tipster."

And then it abruptly cut off, leaving them hanging, the air thick with anticipation. The tip held vital information—a piece of the puzzle they needed more than ever to crack open the case of this stolen document. But the meeting was to take place in a deserted parking lot in the dead of night.

"We must be very careful," cautioned Brett in a low, gravelly voice. "It might be a trap."

Emma looked at him, her eyes fierce and full of determination. "We can't afford to be scared, Brett. We have to do this; this is our opening to blow this one wide open."

The parking lot was dark and empty, filled with old, rusty cars. A figure, a hooded man holding onto a manila envelope in the clutch of his hands, came out of the darkness. As Brett came closer, a hand instinctively going towards the weapon he carried, Emma kept watch, her senses on high alert.

"You're getting too close," the figure's voice echoed out raspily, the hood concealing their words. "Go back before it's too late. Powerful people are involved, and they won't hesitate to silence anyone who gets in their way."

Then, the figure shoved the envelope into Brett's hand and went into the night like a phantom.

The deafening silence filled the car, until they got back to their apartment, only broken by the rhythmic hum of the engine. Brett tore open the envelope, his breath catching in his throat at the sight of the classified documents inside.

"Oh god, Brett," Emma said breathlessly, her eyes wide with excitement and something else, maybe fear. "These papers involve things at the establishment level. We need to take them to the task force at once."

But as they speeded toward headquarters, chilling realizations slowly started to dawn on them. At least not in Neon did the documents say "name." They only suggested it, like the suggestion of a trail of bread crumbs piling up upon itself and then going off thin into some wildly winding maze.

For now, they had stumbled upon something entirely different, something far more sinister than they had ever imagined.

The implications of the documents had initially blown a huge hole in the skepticism of the task force. The investigation escalated, fingers pointed, and accusations flew.

But amidst this chaos, another name emerged, whispered in scared voices: "Hydra," a murky organization whose tentacles reached into the highest echelons of power. Fear gnawed at them, for they knew powerful forces were aware of their machinations now. They were no longer mere investigators; they had become targets for elimination. But the truth was a siren song whose seductive melody no one could refuse.

***

The newsroom at the Capitol Tribune was buzzing with the never-ending hum of lights—the symphony of Emma's never-ending quest for truth. Her fingers danced on the keyboard, telling the story of corruption with a nimble deftness that only an investigative journalist, whose skills had been well practiced and honed, could exercise.

Tonight it wasn't about some sleazebag businessman; tonight, it was a secret group within the power elite of D.C., so their tentacles reached right up into the top offices of power.

A notification on her screen made her heart stop. An anonymous source had code-named themselves "Deep throat" and dropped a digital breadcrumb. The cryptic yet dire message referred to a "capitol conspiracy," with a whisper of Senators and House Members being involved in the high-stakes game, along with some hint of Chinese government involvement. Each word was a lit match thrown into a tinderbox of secrets.

"Brett," she mumbled, dialing his number as she pushed the encrypted message across her desk. "Meet me at the usual place. We've got a problem."

Minutes later, in the dimly lit café, there was Brett—her lover, a man whose connections reached out far and plunged into some very black shadows. If even the aroma of fresh coffee could describe the tension that hung almost physically in the air, it would not compare to how sharply it bit when he sat across from her in the booth.

"Who put a bee in your bonnet, tiger?" he asked, his voice all serious.

Emma shoved the phone across the table. "Read this."

Brett's brow furrowed as he scanned the message. "Foreign powers? This is getting bigger than we ever imagined, Emma. Exposing this could be explosive."

Her eyes never leaving his, as she says, "I know, but we can't just brush it under the rug, Brett. We need to find this congressman and work out what the hell's going on with the Chinese."

The silence turned tense, only broken by the sound of spoons hitting against ceramic mugs. They were bearing the burden of the situation, like a government secret.

Finally, Brett said in a low voice, "I'll reach out to my people. Of course, very discreetly. We need a name for this congressman; track down that email. If this thing's real, it could be our smoking gun."

It was in these passing days—blurring into nights—that their investigation had taken them yet deeper into the political swamp. Dark trails of money, cryptic messages, and whispers of influence peddling. It felt like threading through a minefield on every step, with every corner holding another trap.

One evening, Brett asked, "Do you think Morrison is the guy?" His face was lit by the flickering light of the laptop screen filled with financial records.

"He's got the ties, the history," Emma said, tapping away at her keyboard. "But something's missing. We need something concrete, something you can't deny."

The answer lay somewhere submerged within the heart of the Capitol—a truth to be exhumed. A dance with darkness, life, or death is the prize.

Sometime later in the same evening, while she was looking through mountains of documents, one detail caught Emma's attention. "Hey, wait a minute," she said, pointing at a redacted section in the middle of a report. "Here, it says that there is a meeting between Morrison and a Chinese operative by the name of Li Wei. Could that be our email?"

Brett leaned over, reading the report. "That's certainly plausible. But that email is something we are going to have to wrestle from him, Emma. We need to get our hands on that email, and that means getting very close to Morrison."

That brought a stubborn smile to Emma's lips. "Deal, but we have to be careful, Brett. We're playing with fire here."

He looked at her, his eyes filled with a mixture of apprehension and admiration. "Always," he replied.

Across the table, their hands met, and they shared a silent pact in facing the danger. Started just right now with The Capitol Conspiracy; that dance with darkness was making the first steps. Everything they do and everything they talk about, can be the last for them. But when pushing for the truth, sometimes, you just have to walk right into the fire.

*****

The crystal chandeliers at the charity gala dripped brilliance onto the silhouette of Emma's elegance in a halo of shimmering light, her heart beating out the counterpoint to the string quartet—not from the music but from the man she was about to confront. Congressman James Morrison, as smooth as a smile and guarded as a vault, was her quarry tonight.

"Congressman Morrison," she purred, her voice a practiced melody of charm. "I am delighted to meet you. That recent bill of yours on renewable energy is quite impressive."

His smile faltered for a moment, a hint of suspicion crossing his eyes. "Thank you, Ms.?"

"Emma," she said, taking his hand. "From the Capitol Tribune."

Their talk was a careful dance, each step full of ulterior motives. Emma, her every sense peeled for some chink in his armor, subtly dropped questions in the hope of snaring a nugget of truth. Morrison, deflecting like a seasoned pro, offered PR-perfect answers, revealing nothing.

But Emma's eyes had sparked with the triumph of catching him stealing a glance at his phone to exchange something brief with a man she recognized—the Chinese diplomat Li Wei. She took a picture on the phone when she did it surreptitiously, like a silent accusation waiting to be launched from its medium.

"Well, Congressman," she grinned the veiled steel in her voice, "it's been real. But duty calls."

Later, in the dim newsroom, Emma and Brett bent over the photo from the gala like two detectives wrangling a piece of evidence in a murder investigation.

"He's meeting with Li Wei," Brett said, his timeless deadpan eyes sharpening as if that fact itself were breaking news. "What else could they possibly have to do with each other, Emma?"

"More than we know," she said, fingers flying across the keyboard. "But this gala wasn't just for schmoozing. It was a signal, a confirmation of something bigger."

"We're ready to go," the words from the email Emma took a picture of whispered in their heads. This was more than stolen documentation. It was turning out to be a clandestine operation, a labyrinth of corruption running far and wide, implicating them with more than Morrison's bought vote.

"We need to find out what 'ready to go' means, Brett," she said, urgency lacing her voice. "It's the key to figuring out this whole mess."

The investigation took on a new urgency; they traced trails of dark money, cryptic messages, and whispers of influence. And he was not the only one. In fact, others were part of a broader conspiracy. The gala picture became an indispensable piece, a clue to unweave the net.

Every day turned into a trail that never waited. Every discovery was another step closer to the truth, every step deeper into danger. The Capitol was no more than just another seat of power; it was a battleground where secrets danced with shadows and any conversation spelled danger.

***

The printer sounded like a small plane in the middle of the night, taking off as it hummed to life and started printing all the documents Emma fed into it, one by one.

Across the kitchen table, Brett had an identical, concentrated frown on his forehead, a sharp glance going over a pile of reports. The edge of tension was there; it was not spoken, never forgotten by the dangerous dance they always had to tread.

A sharp knock at the door shattered the quietness. Emma's head shot up, and the frown of concentration was erased from its place. Brett automatically reached for his holstered weapon and moved to the peephole, dread washing over him when he saw two figures and the sunglasses that concealed their faces.

"Honey," he grimly whispered low, "we have company. I think they've found us."

Her heart nearly jumped into her throat, fluttering madly like a caged bird. "What do we do, Brett?" she breathed, just raising the volume of her voice.

Panic started to rise in Brett's calm eyes as they looked into each other's eyes. "We stick together, Emma. And we find a way out of this."

His voice had faded away into the heavy silence from outside, filled with anticipation.

The two figures at the door started banging, muffled but insistent, their demands reaching through the door. Brett looked at the back door, his mind racing.

"Emma," he rasped quietly, "grab that hard drive. We need it."

She grabbed the hard drive. Adrenaline made her limbs shake as she pushed the chair back, scattering paperwork and folders all over the table, her trembling hand scrambling over the surface in an attempt to find the small black device that would contain all their investigation.

Brett's hand closed around the pistol in his pocket. "Stay behind me, ready to run. when I say."

He moved like a silent predator, his steps light and measured. Reaching the door, he unlocked it with a quick click. The men outside surged forward, pushing their way into the dimly lit room.

Brett answered instantly, "Federal agents! Freeze!" and his voice was sharp and commanding. But the intruders hesitated only a heartbeat, their faces set in surprised anger.

"He's bluffing," one growled, going for a weapon hidden under his jacket. In that fraction of a second, the room turned into a war zone. Brett fired, and the sound echoed in the confined space.

One of the intruders went down, an arm clutched to his side. The other hesitated, stunned for a moment.

"Now!" Brett bellowed with urgency. They darted for the exit at the back and frantically scrambled through the sparsely lit apartment. Hot on their heels, the heavy footsteps of the men echoed ahead of them off the wooden floor.

They burst out onto the patio, the cool night air shocking against their sweat-pricked skin. Emma's lungs felt on fire with her effort, but she dared not look back. In front of them loomed the fence—a daunting obstacle.

"Over!" Brett urged, breaking into a run and soaring over the top of the wooden barrier. Emma followed, her foot catching on the edge, and she tumbled to the ground. Pain shot through her ankle, but she ignored it and scrambled to her feet. They sprinted across the moonlit yard, the men's shouts growing fainter with each desperate stride.

They reached the darkness of the alley, a welcome shroud. Panting, they huddled in the shadow, the adrenaline leaving them shaking.

"We can't stay here," Brett said, his voice a ragged whisper.

Emma nodded, her mind racing. "Safe house?"

"Too risky. We need to disappear. Regroup."

They moved through the city like wraiths, weaving the knowledge of secret alleyways and forgotten shortcuts to shake their tails. Finally, they arrived at a dingy apartment building, a preordained haven known to none but those well within Brett's circle.

The air was stale inside, heavily mingled with dust and neglect. But it was safe.

"Hydra," the name of that insidious body, they were tracking, rolled on the tip of her tongue, leaving the flavor as if it were ash.

Brett's jaw tightened. "I told you not to worry, Emma. They won't stop us. We're bringing them out into the light."

That dim haven was a spark of new resolve within. The close call had been an awakening, brutally bringing them back to reality, but they wouldn't let that prove a deterrent. It was the dangerous beginning of the cat-and-mouse games with Hydra, and now the stakes just went higher. They had a story to tell and a truth to reveal, and they wouldn't rest until that darkness was brought to light by God.

Chapter Ten:
The Spy In The Shadows

The oil lamp flickered and threw long, distorted shadows on the faces of the gathering assembled in the secret chamber below the Capitol.

Senator Robbins had his eyes glinting like a predator in the darkness, tapping a long, bony finger against the worn leather tabletop. "The woman, Emma Hayes," he rasped, his voice weighted with menace. "She's become a thorn in our side, a pesky journalist sniffing too close to the truth. We need to silence her permanently."

Congressman Morrison shifted uncomfortably. His face was white against the darkness. "But Senator, are we sure we cannot simply reason with her and offer her a heavy sum to depart? Surely even a journalist has a price."

There was a cold, humorless chuckle from the corner where Fixer was sitting—hardly seen because of the darkness there. But his chuckle was famous, and so were the solutions he had offered to several problems—all very discreet ones. "No, gentlemen. Not this time. We need to send a message, a warning, to anyone who dares to cross our path. A public spectacle, swift and brutal."

The Fixer leaned forward, and it seemed to them that his eyes sparkled like two predatory stars. "Imagine the headlines: 'Renowned journalist found dead; investigation ongoing.' A chilling reminder of the consequences for those who pry too deep."

An oppressive silence fell into the room—so much so that the creaking of the floorboards seemed very nervous in the situation. Then, the weight of the fixer's words landed on their shoulders— something as heavy as the secrets that they guarded.

"But what about Evans?" Morrison finally choked out, his voice a mere tremor. "He won't just sit idly by while his lover disappears."

Robbins sneered, twisting his lips cruelly. "Of course, Evans is next, of course. But first, let the death of Hayes be a lesson—a public execution staged to shatter his resolve. Once he's broken, dealing with him will be child's play."

A murmur of fear washed through the room. They knew the Fixer would be the first to see the plan through despite its harshness. But to actually think of the act—that one would have to silence an innocent woman or put a leading journalist in darkness—was chilling.

"Are we certain that this is the only way?" Morrison pressed, barely taking a breath.

The fixer squinted his eyes. "Got a better one, Congressman? One that doesn't leave blood on the floor?"

Morrison clamped his mouth shut so tightly that his face turned into a mask of a mixture of fear and defiance. He knew, he was not turning back. The die had been cast, the curtains drawn on a deadly game of cat and mouse where life and death were the stakes, and from the shadows watched silent and knowing.

***

The Fixer stalked up and down, restless, his eyes glinting happily as panthers. Senator Morrison and the Hydra, lost in the darkness, leaned forward towards him, though their faces vanished in blackness, and their greed was perfectly visible. In the secret back room, with little and very dim lights, each word spoken now produced a conspiracy.

"Operation Blue Orchid," the fixer snarled, his voice cold and precise. "Elegant, untraceable, and perfectly timed."

He enunciated, what he had in mind: a deadly orchid genetically altered to launch a needle of poison—the deadly assassin hidden behind the mask of beauty. The object of their operation was Emma, the indomitable journalist who, through her continued pursuit, had thrown a gauntlet at their corrupt destiny.

That night, a ghost of theirs, also known as the henchman, sneaked into Emma's favorite greenhouse. He coolly placed the orchid with practiced hands in between her prized blooms, the starkly purple orchid appearing almost offensive amidst the pure white of innocent lilies.

The next morning, unaware of the danger hiding in its beauty, Emma reached out, and her fingers caressed the fragile petals.

A microscopic needle, buried in the heart of the deadly orchid, sprang to life. A droplet of poison, deadly and untraceable, ran through her veins. It was the first creeping tendrils of weakness, so insidious in nature, a faint fatigue she associated with long nights and the driving pursuit to find the truth.

Brett, the lover, confidant, and shadow of Emma's soul, observed as worry etched deeper lines into Emma's brow. Emma's usually bright eyes dulled, reflecting the exhaustion that clung to her like a shroud.

He softly uttered, "Em," concern lacing his voice. His thumb reached out, brushing away a stray tear that escaped down her cheek. The gesture posed a silent question, inviting her to share the burden she carried.

Emma managed a watery smile, its fragility breaking Brett's heart. Her voice was rough at the edges, and she rasped, "Just a long day, love."

Seeing through her facade, Brett recognized the subtle signs of a deeper struggle, knowing Emma too well. He slid his arm around her shoulders, pulling her close, and finding solace in the familiar scent of her shampoo.

Relieved by his embrace, Emma sank into it, feeling the tension in her shoulders finally ease. A shaky breath escaped her, lost amidst the warmth emanating from Brett's chest. In that tranquil haven, the weight of the world seemed to recede, replaced by the comforting stability of his presence.

Brett tilted his chin, his lips hovering just a whisper away from hers. With a touch as light as a feather, he conveyed his unspoken question. Responding to the unyielding affection in his eyes, Emma closed the distance, their lips meeting in a kiss that sought solace and reassurance. The love and worry intertwining within them spoke volumes, an unspoken pledge to support one another in the face of the impending storm.

The kiss deepened, a languid exploration revealing the depth of their unspoken affections. Brett's hand meandered down Emma's back, eliciting a shiver of awareness. However, their burgeoning desire was abruptly interrupted by a sharp cough that tore through Emma's lips, shattering their shared fragile moment.

Emma pulled away, her features twisted in a grimace of discomfort. Shame flushed her cheeks as she hastily wiped her mouth with the back of her hand. She whispered, her voice laden with remorse, "Sorry, this stupid cough..."

Cupping her face, Brett's touch was gentle yet resolute. He murmured, his gaze unwaveringly locked with hers, "Don't apologize." His thumb tenderly brushed away a fresh tear trailing down her cheek. He reassured her, his voice husky with unspoken desire, "We can wait. Your health is of utmost importance."

Emma's eyes flickered with disappointment, but gratitude swiftly replaced it. Leaning into his touch, she found solace in his unwavering concern. For now, the comfort of his presence provided solace, silently promising that they would confront whatever darkness lay ahead, hand in hand.

Conspirators, the lot of them, were glued to the screens of hidden cameras like they were enjoying her struggle. "You see, Senator," the Fixer purred, pure malice lacing each word. "She won't be a problem much longer. And Brett." A cruel smile twisted his lips. "He'll watch her fade, helpless to stop it."

But the silent message was the most stultifying of all: their power was absolute, their will wielded in every quarter, and their hands kept the whole world at bay. Yet the game had just begun, and Brett never had a lot of patience for giving in to shadows.

***

A stark, heavy, sterile stench of disinfectant filled the air—so perfectly contrasting the frantic beat of Emma's heart monitor. Her expressionless and pallid face against the white—so white it was almost blinding—sheets held a portentous stillness that seemed to be shredding at his very soul. The doctors had no answers for him, and in that sea of uncertainty and fear, Brett was drowning.

"Emma," he said in a pleadingly thick voice. "Wake up, please. We've got a lot of stuff still left to go over, remember?"

Silence.

Met only by the beeping of the monitor, a metronome mocking his desperation. Brett remembered checking the camera footage of the greenhouse. He remembered the orchid—an exotic beauty blooming in her backyard greenhouse. The bizarre gift, of course, was delivered anonymously just weeks before her illness. His gut churned, suspicion slowly coiling tighter and tighter.

"It wasn't an accident," he whispered, more to himself than to the seemingly unconscious Emma. "She was silenced. Somebody wanted her silenced."

Instinct kicked in, fine-tuned from years spent in the shadows. This was no heartbreak; it was a case to crack. He wouldn't let her fade into that good night without a fight. So, under the cover of the darkness, he sneaked out of the hospital and back into Emma's greenhouse.

The air hung heavy with that cloying smell of the orchid; a silent accusation. He looked at the plant with his well-trained eyes, scouring it for any clues that may have been left behind. The faint prick on a leaf, the small puncture mark—the key, he'd searched for so long.

His phone buzzed, and from a source known only to him, he read two words: "Orchid. Chinese lab. Classified research. silenced." Chilling bits of the puzzle come together into a chilling picture of betrayal and deceit.

Back in his secret safe house, a steely resolve masked the seething. He leaned closer to a trusted hacker, lowering his voice. "Get me everything on that orchid—where it came from, its properties. I want to know who sent it and why."

Days became nights, and he dug deeper, the walls of his world shrinking to fit the confines of the investigation. He grilled informants, ran after rumors down shadowy alleyways, and tried to make his way through a bureaucratic obstacle course. Every step was a gamble, and every piece of information was a potential death sentence.

Finally, the big break: the genetically modified orchid was a rare flower, host to some or other toxin, and it had originated from a super-secret Chinese research facility.

The target: Emma and everybody they believed to be unfriendly to their cause.

He tasted the truth in his mouth, burning like ash. Emma, his love, was situated in the geopolitical game crossfire that he barely understood. Surrender was not on the cards. He could not let the shadows win.

He had a plan—a desperately wild gamble fueled by both love and vengeance. He was to reveal, no, eviscerate, the conspiracy, piece by piece.

The orchid was to be a weapon, a sign of treachery. He was to make the poison's own antidote and turn the tables on the manufacturer.

Brett remembered his last visit by her bedside, cloaked in the hush of the dawn. Her eyes fluttered open, weak but boundless with determination. "Brett," she rasped, her breath making a whisper of sound.

He took her hand; his touch was a promise. "I'm here, Emma. And we're going to fight this together."

Her lips curled in a flicker of a defiant smile. "Of course we are, Brett. Let's show them what happens, when they mess with the wrong people."

But right now, machines whirred with a more even rhythm than even the silence between her and Brett. He had not left her since he got the news of the bioengineered orchid and its deadly toxin singing loud in his ears.

"It's too late to do anything else," the doctor had told them; the tone had been so heavy, full of the weight of the world and remorse, in his voice. "The poison is acting too fast."

Brett wouldn't accept that. Holding her hand, he interlaced his fingers with hers as though beseeching them to offer even a spark of warmth or some reaction.

"Come on, Emma," he urged in an incendiary whisper, his voice raw. "Fight it. Be strong. Remember?"

But she'd just laid there, eyes closed, the rise and fall of her chest almost imperceptible. Each tortured, laboring inhalation was a knife further turning in his gut.

He was startled by a knock on the door, and in walked their unlikely ally in this fight, a botanist with a grim face.

"I found where that orchid comes from," he said in a lowered voice. "Secret lab, financed by a secret organization. They call themselves the Garden of Shadows."

Brett narrowed his eyes. "Garden of Shadows," he repeated, savoring the word. "And they're the ones who poisoned Emma?"

The botanist nodded, his eyes filled with sorrow. "Yes, that would be the case," he said. "They probably wanted to keep the girl quiet and anyone else who got close to the matter."

Grief threatened to consume him, but he pushed it down, hardening the resolve into a cold, steely determination. "Then, they have made a mistake," he growled low and dangerously. "They have awakened a storm."

He turned back to Emma, watching the vitality in her life deplete with each passing tick of the clock. "I'm not going to let them get away with this, Emma," he whispered, his voice thick with emotion. "I'm going to reveal them for what they really are, rip their Garden of Shadows all the way to the ground, and I'm going to make sure they're going to pay for what they did to you."

A tear ran over his eyes and down his cheek. He leaned in, and his lips brushed hers. "I love you, Emma," he said. "And I promise, your death will not go unavenged."

The machine flat-lined, and a chilling calm filled Brett. Love turned to fury and blazed within him for Emma. He wouldn't bring the Garden of Shadows down; he'd have to bring it crashing down, tearing apart their operation piece by piece.

He left the hospital; the cold of the night air bit through to replace the sterile white walls. There was only one thing on the mind of the driver, which, he considered the most needed at the time—revenge and justice. The Garden of Shadows had overstepped. They had thought it was silencing a reporter, but much worse—they had let something else out: a man inexorable, with nothing to lose, and love with raw fury for weapons.

The whole game had taken a 180-degree spin. It was not only an investigation now; it was personal against him. A lethal lone wolf, grief heaped on his heart as a heavy burden, and an angry flame licked away at his soul, who was after them. The Garden of Shadows had played their hand but certainly didn't contemplate the storm they had unleashed so casually. And in the coming darkness, Brett was going to be their very own justice.

***

Within the halls of Capitol Hill, twisty with hidden passages, whispers of a phantom moved across the cold current. Chinese operative Mei glided over the treacherous landscape with all the poise of a viper and the smarts of a fox.

Her assignment: Congressman James Morrison, one of the wealthy, influential men whose secrets held a trump card to the shaping of the world. Mei was actually playing the part of the quiet and shy legislative assistant, Mei Ling, but it would soon become quite apparent to all of them that her true self was a whole lot deadlier than that.

She had mastered the art of deception, poising from the sculpted porcelain of her features and having a smile that could disarm even the iciest of facades. And with a mind that had been trained for years, it could be let out once she put it to use. Each step was a poised dance that had been calculated on the razor's edge of ambition against anonymity.

Now, one can see how that put Mei in a bit of a predicament— one little lonely body in that big Congressman's office, with the briefest click of her keyboard, unlocking a secret compartment to reveal those nefarious, classified documents.

A drumbeat against her ribs, the constant thrum of anticipation. Then the door creaked open. A face wearies and worn on the edges that of Congressman Morrison came through first. Mei snapped the compartment shut, a mask of innocence sliding down over her features.

"Still working late, Mei Ling?" he said in that tone that held suspicion at its center.

"Just finalizing some reports, sir," she said with a newfound steadiness in her voice. Morrison's eyes bored into her for a moment, a bit too long, as though to find some hint of treachery, but Mei did not move. Her poker face was perfect. He gave an exasperated sigh and looked away.

"Fine. Just make sure to be discreet."

His words hung silently in the air as if they were a warning. Mei knew just what risks she ran and how fragile that game, which she toyed with, was. One foot out of place, one word misspoken, and she could ravel it—her life, so carefully built, and smashing it.

But with it came, the heady intoxication of the game and of the power she held in her palm. Every purloined document, every secret dropped in whispers, was a weapon with which, she could hold the world at bay. That night, in her apartment, she decrypted the files. With her eyes wide, she read; the things of which that information spoke brought a chill even deeper than the coldness of the room to her very marrow. This was not political manipulation; it was a game of global chess, pitting lives and countries against each other as pawns.

Knowledge of its weight pressed into her; that burden was heavier than her mind could think up. But it was known. She couldn't turn her back. The game had taken hold of her, and now it would play through until it ended. Her loyalty would be tested, and it would mean her life. The dance went on, Mei a ghost in the halls of power, every movement a calculus of chance. The line between spy and traitor began to blur, and her secrets were turning into a time bomb that just kept on ticking away. In this political cauldron, Mei, the enigma in silk, would rise to be either the master of the game or its ultimate victim.

***

One afternoon, while asked to get coffee for the Congressman, Mei overheard a rather heated conversation that he had over the phone. It seemed that it sounded like one of those days when he was in a bad mood.

"The deal is almost sealed," said the baritone voice of Morrison from behind the door. "The project is about to be completed."

Her heart throbbed in her chest. Project? What deal was he talking about? Curiosity worked with the fear that mounted much stronger in her belly, but she had to take that risk.

Much later in the night, while organizing his files, Mei saw her chance. "Congressman," she started, casual in her fake inquiry, "I couldn't help but overhear you earlier—about that project, I mean. Is there any way I can help?"

Morrison squinted his eyes, suspicion flitting across his face. "No, Mei Ling. That's not for you to concern yourself with. I made it clear that I expected your attention to be on your tasks."

"Of course, sir," she said, firm in her respect, "but I am always a zealous learner and contributor within the realms of propriety."

The congressman looked at her for a beat, then sighed with sudden impatience. "Alright. There's this project that is about to be completed soon. Something related to sensitive materials. Discretion is key; do you get me?"

And Mei's pulse raced. There it was, and she saw her chance: that little crack in Morrison's burly front. "Yes, sir," she said as her mind whirled over the possibilities.

It was a short conversation, but it had opened a door. Mei had sown the seed of trust, and she would tend to it very carefully and hope and pray that the thing might grow into a lifeline towards the heart of the conspiracy. That's if the game hadn't just gone far deeper than, they ever could have anticipated, and the stakes were now astronomically higher. But Mei, a viper in silk, was prepared to play.

***

The glittering lights of the office hid the false sheen on Congressman James Morrison's carefully constructed life. At the top of American ambition—young, charismatic, and popular—he had been the embodiment of the American dream. He had a dutiful wife, a big home, and integrity that reached from coast to coast and greased the way for his dream—the Oval Office.

But behind the facade, there lay shadows. Morrison, with his never-satisfied appetite for more power and wealth, allowed himself to be a constant victim of temptation.

Enter Mei Ling, the alluring enigma that hid secrets behind that beautiful face and unblemished Mandarin. Placed there by a bought-off security staffer, she was not just an assistant under a veil but also the all-seeing, all-hearing eyes and ears of the Chinese government within the American political machine.

"From today on, you'll be my confidante, Mei," Morrison purred, unaware of the viper he was nurturing in his bosom. "Discreet, of course. My eyes and ears, when I can't be everywhere."

Mei's answer was a sharp-toothed smile and the words, "Always, Congressman. Your trust is my honor."

But every interaction to follow had the quality of something out of a carefully orchestrated dance. While Mei scrupulously managed his schedule, she also perused documents with a practiced eye, glided through emails with a ghostly touch, and took pictures of classified materials hidden from view with a camera that didn't look like anything more than a pen. Information. Each pilfered piece was a weapon to be used against the heart of American security.

***

The Washington twilight cast long shadows across Congressman Morrison's office, mirroring the secrets hidden within its mahogany walls. Mei Ling, the picture of diligent efficiency, meticulously organized her boss's schedule. But beneath her calm exterior, a storm raged. She wasn't just an assistant; she was a viper in silk, a Chinese operative on a mission to steal America's secrets.

Tonight, opportunity slithered in with the setting sun. Morrison, preoccupied with an upcoming summit, left his office unattended. Mei's heart hammered a frantic rhythm against her ribs as she approached his desk, her movements swift and silent. Her nimble fingers danced across the keyboard, unlocking a hidden compartment. Inside, a manila envelope pulsed with classified documents.

One file slipped easily out of the pile, and she glanced at the title: "Project Ghost-walker." A shiver ran down her back. This wasn't a new political ploy; it was a game-changer, a blueprint for robotic soldiers that could shift the global balance of power.

Suddenly, the door creaked open. There was Morrison, with a tired face, greeted by lines. Mei's world stood still. Her hand hung over the file, her mute accusation hanging in the air.

"Mei Ling," Morrison sighed, his voice laced with suspicion as he eyed the contents. "Working late again?"

"Just finishing up, sir," she replied smoothly, though her mind was doing backflips at this point. Think, Mei Ling, think!

"I noticed the files," Morrison continued, now narrowing his eyes. "Anything sensitive?"

Her mind spun a web of lies. "Just routine reports, Congressman. Nothing for your concern."

A tense silence stretched between them, thicker even than the humid Washington air. At last, Morrison shook his head and retreated, the door clicking shut behind him. Mei exhaled, air slipping out in a shaky breath.

The close call sent adrenaline coursing through her veins. Alone, back in the quiet of her apartment, she devoured the file of the ghost-walker. Every detail was a revelation—one piece of a puzzle that showed her a world of secret and covert operations with advanced weaponry. Such information was nothing but a treasure for China. It was her weapon; it gave her the power to rewrite the rules of the game.

Chapter Eleven:
Dark Web Of Espionage

The room buzzed softly as a soft whirl filled with computers of unimaginable strength. Dragon, a man whose age was obscured by years of experience etched into his face, scanned data projected by a holographic screen over a solid desktop before him. His brows furrowed, and his fingers began dancing over the virtual keyboard.

"Any progress, my friend?" A deep voice boomed from the corner. A massive man, only known as Tiger, appeared out of the shadows, his eyes riveted upon the labyrinthine formulations scrolling across the screen.

Dragon shook his head, his frustration evident. "The encryption is complex, even for our best algorithms. But Mei Ling wouldn't send a message like this unless it was critical."

Tiger grunted in agreement. "She's the best, we have on the inside. Loyal, cunning, and discreet." He paused, his gaze flickering towards a photo on the wall—a young woman, Mei Ling, her smile radiating warmth and intelligence. "I just pray she hasn't been compromised."

A tense silence settled in the room, broken only by the rhythmic hum of the computers. Dragon exhaled, his voice steeled with resolve. "We can't afford to lose focus. Keep running decryption protocols. I need everyone at their best."

Across the globe, in the opulent office of Congressman Morrison, a different kind of tension brewed. Mei Ling paced around the room, reviewing a stack of classified documents with meticulous attention. She was dressed and poised with immaculate precision. Her heart was pounding against her ribs so hard that it almost hurt, in contrast to the calm exterior she gave the world.

"Anything interesting, Ms. Ling?" Congressman Morrison inquired, his voice laced with a hint of flirtation.

Mei Ling forced a smile, her mind racing as she searched for the data she needed. "Just a few routine reports, Mr. Congressman. There is nothing that requires your immediate attention."

A sly grin spread across Morrison's face. "I trust you'll alert me if anything urgent arises." He leaned closer, his voice dropping to a husky whisper. "We have an understanding, don't we?"

Mei Ling swallowed the lump in her throat, her stomach churning with a mix of guilt and fear. "Of course, Mr. Congressman. Your priorities are my top concern."

As Morrison retreated behind a stack of paperwork, Mei Ling felt a pang of unease. The line between her duty to her country and the man she was coming to care for blurred with each passing day. She knew, she had to extract the information soon before her loyalties became an even greater burden.

***

We have a partial decryption!
We have a partial decryption!
We have a partial decryption!

The tension in the room remained palpable as Dragon and his team relentlessly tried to unlock the encryption. Hours bled into days, fatigue gnawing at the edges of their concentration. Finally, a notification blared on a central monitor, sending a jolt of energy through the team.

"We have a partial decryption!" a young team member, codenamed Sparrow, exclaimed, her voice trembling with excitement.

Dragon leaned in, scrutinizing the newly revealed data. Lines of complex code unfurled before him, slowly revealing fragments of classified information. His eyes widened as he recognized a string of keywords: "B-21 next-gen" and "Project Horizon: AI Integration."

"My comrades," Dragon announced, his voice resonating with a mixture of awe and trepidation, "we've stumbled upon something far bigger than we ever imagined, A miracle"

He explained the information they had managed to extract; his words painted a chilling picture. The Americans were not only developing a new generation of stealth bombers but also a fleet of robotic soldiers powered by artificial intelligence. The implications were staggering. These advancements could tip the global power balance significantly, and Dragon knew they had to act fast.

"We need to get this information to our superiors immediately," he declared, his gaze resolute. "The potential ramifications of this project are too immense to ignore."

Tiger, ever the pragmatist, chimed in, "But sending the full data is too risky. We don't know how much Mei Ling has managed to extract, and raising suspicion at this point could jeopardize the entire operation."

A silence of consideration fell on the room as to what was the best thing to do. Sparrow, with a mind hard at work, ventured, "What if we send a redacted version, focusing only on the most critical aspects? We can frame it as a potential leak from a different source, diverting suspicion from Mei Ling."

Dragon took a moment to dwell on what she had said, and reckon the odds and the benefits crossed his mind. At last, he nodded in agreement and said, "Sparrow, you are right; there should be extreme caution, but, sorry to say, everything cannot be clear. Prepare that report of deduction, and I will try to send it to our heads through all available channels."

As the team scrambled into action, the air in the room filled with a sense of urgency. It was indeed a moment not to be forgotten by them—that they were at a groundbreaking proximity, and every step forward weighted heavily with such discovery. So much seemed to hang at that moment—perhaps even the fate of their nation and possibly the world.

***

With measured care, Mei Ling methodically went through the ream of classified documents. The weight of her deception pressed heavily, and yet she held her external demeanor together as if nothing was wrong; her heart raged to escape her chest at any moment. The information she sought—the key to unraveling Project Horizon—remained frustratingly elusive.

Across the secure communication line, her handler, codenamed Dragon, awaited her update. "Anything, Mei Ling?" His voice crackled with a hint of urgency.

"Not yet," she replied, her voice strained. "Security has been tightened in the wake of recent data breaches. Every access point is heavily monitored."

The dragon cursed under his breath. "We can't afford any delays. The information you bring is critical."

A determined glint flickered in Mei Ling's eyes. "I understand. Don't worry, Dragon. I'll find a way."

The following days were a blur of meticulous planning and calculated risks. Mei Ling observed the new security protocols, her mind working tirelessly to find a loophole. She noticed a slight discrepancy in the access codes for a specific server, a vulnerability she could potentially exploit.

Late one evening, after everyone had left the office, Mei Ling pretended that she had to get some files from the server room. As she was at the usual access code entry keypad, she hovered her fingers for a microsecond and then gave it a calculated entry such that she entered a code similar to what any other person would have but different in a way she designed closely after observation.

The tension was coiling tighter in her stomach as it hissed, the electrically stoked smooth hiss of the system, a taut silence following through. And then, on the screen, a green light flickered, and it opened.

Instant relief flooded through her, causing adrenaline to flood through her immediately after. She was running out of time. Her fingers practically flew over the keys, downloading and then quickly compressing the most urgent data with regard to Project Horizon.

Every second seemed like an eternity. A staccato beat against her chest—the sound of her pumping heart.

Scarcely had she finished downloading, when there was a sound from down the barren hallway—one that set her heart up into her throat. Someone was coming. She scrambled to shut everything down and get out of the server room, moving with practiced efficiency in a blur of motion.

As she emerged, her face calmed and set back into its professional lines, but she almost ran into a security guard making his rounds. He cast her a suspicious glance.

"Is everything alright here, Ms. Ling?" he inquired, his voice gruff.

Mei Ling forced a smile; her voice was calm and reassuring. "I'm just finishing up some late paperwork. Thank you for keeping a watchful eye, Mr. Jones."

The guard nodded curtly, his suspicion seemingly abating. When he was well out of earshot, Mei Ling let out a shaky breath, still trembling; her body thrumming with adrenaline. She had managed to recover some of the data, but certainly not all of it; there was still a whole lot of work to be done for this mission. Time was fast running out, and the stakes were at their highest.

***

Mei Ling felt a pang of guilt as Congressman Morrison left his office after a long day at work, oblivious to the encrypted message waiting in his secure inbox. Her handlers had set up a prolific ghost series of servers to route him a communication in code, but it was the contents of the elaborately encoded message that made her stomach roll. She wasn't receiving information anymore; she was interacting with orders that spelled out exactly how she was supposed to coerce Congressman Morrison to operate against the interests of the United States.

It was a cocktail of feelings swirling inside her. Loyalty to the home country deep down, she would always be reminded of sacrifices made to get her there thus far. And yet, over the past year, an unexpected bond has formed with Congressman Morrison. Witnessing his dedication to his constituents and his real wish to serve his country, she chipped away at the walls built around her heart. She would now betray a man who had trusted her to that degree.

Duty and love for a traitor intermarried in Mei Ling's heart. These were the weeks through which, she led a double life, walking the treacherous paths of it. So on the outer side, she was the same loyal, unseen aide—the servant devoted, with a large, pleasant smile, always handy and never disarrayed—to give help.

One evening, as they reviewed a particularly sensitive bill, Congressman Morrison reached out, placing a comforting hand on hers. The warmth of his touch sent shivers down her spine, making the lie she lived all the more difficult to bear.

"You're an invaluable asset, Mei Ling," he stated, his gaze sincere. "I don't know what I'd do without your support."

The weight of his words threatened to crush her. How could she betray the man who saw her as a friend, a confidante, or something more? Yet the encrypted message loomed, a constant reminder of the consequences of disobedience.

Later that night, alone in her apartment, Mei Ling activated the hidden compartment within her desk, revealing the secure communication device her handlers had provided. Taking a deep breath, she initiated contact.

"Dragonfly here." Her voice sounded strained even through the voice modulator.

A crackle filled the line, followed by a cold, emotionless voice. "Report, Dragonfly."

With a heavy heart, Mei Ling launched into a carefully worded summary of Morrison's political stances and his growing influence amongst his colleagues. The conversation was brief, devoid of the warmth or empathy she secretly craved. Yet, the task was done. She had crossed a line, becoming not just a spy but a manipulator, a pawn in a game far bigger than herself.

As she hung up, tears were barely falling. A single one fell noiselessly on a picture of her as a hopeful and innocent girl, not knowing that one day she would become a woman hopelessly torn between two worlds, tortured by the choices she had to make.

***

Despite the turmoil within, Mei Ling knew that she had to continue her mission. The weight of her secret gnawed at her, but revealing the truth would have disastrous consequences. So, she employed the weapon her handlers had honed—her seductive charm.

Over the next few weeks, the subtle dance of seduction intensified. Late nights spent poring over legislation turned into lingering touches; shared glances were exchanged across the conference table. Mei Ling, skilled in the art of deception, fueled Morrison's growing infatuation.

It was a Monday evening, and an air of tension crackled in the dimly lit study, but that had nothing to do with the disorderly stacks of bills littered all over the oak desk.

Morrison had pushed back in his chair so forcefully that it nearly toppled over backward, and the knot of his tie was pulling down at the collar of his crisp white shirt. He was rubbing his temples as though pressure might chase the headache away.

Mei Ling sat on the edge of the leather armchair just in front of him with a slight furrowing of her brow and concern on her face.

Her voice, soft and melodic in the quiet room, asked, "Long day?"

Morrison grunted, his eyes still closed. "Feels like I've been wrestling alligators all day."

Mei Ling chuckled gently, gracefully rising and moving to stand behind his chair. Her fingers instinctively reached for his shoulders, lightly brushing against his heated skin, sending a jolt through Morrison. He leaned back slightly, savoring the cool press of her fingertips.

Whispering against his ear, her voice barely audible, she murmured, "Perhaps a massage is in order?"

A shiver ran down his spine as their gazes locked, a silent conversation passing between them. Mei Ling's eyes, usually pools of calculated neutrality, shimmered with a hint of something more. The unspoken invitation hung heavy in the air.

Morrison swallowed, his throat suddenly dry. "Perhaps," he managed, his voice husky.

Mei Ling skillfully began kneading the tension knots in his shoulders, igniting a slow burn within him. The friction of her touch, firm yet gentle, sent tingling jolts down his arm. His eyes closed once more, slowly now, closing with a feeling of relief—tension that slowly dissolved.

In the hushed room, broken only by the rhythmic rustle of paper and Morrison's soft breaths, Mei Ling leaned closer, her warm breath caressing his ear.

"You're working too hard, Senator," she murmured, her voice a barely audible whisper.

Morrison tilted his head slightly, his lips gently brushing against her cheek. Desire surged within him, the urge to pull her closer, to explore the burgeoning connection between them.

However, their intimate moment was abruptly interrupted by a knock on the study door, startling them both. Mei Ling stepped back, a faint smile playing on her lips.

Morrison, his voice gruff, called out, "Come in."

The door creaked open, revealing a young intern holding a stack of files. The fleeting intimacy dissolved, leaving behind a lingering tension, and a yearning for something more. The subtle dance of seduction had begun.

In the same week, as they reviewed a particularly sensitive document, her hand brushed against his. Startled, he looked up, his eyes searching hers. The moment hung heavy in the air, a silent plea for something more.

"Jim," she began, her voice barely a whisper, using his first name for the first time. "I... I care about you more than just an assistant."

His heart pounded in his chest. This was a line he had never expected her to cross. Before he could respond, she continued, her voice trembling slightly. "But I have a secret, Jim. A secret that could ruin everything."

Intrigued and confused, Morrison leaned closer. Her next words shattered his world.

"I'm not who you think I am," she confessed, her voice a mere shadow of its usual confident tone. "I work for the Chinese government. And I need your help."

She revealed the encrypted message, detailing her mission and the consequences of refusal. Fear and betrayal flooded Morrison's mind. His trusted confidante, the woman he had grown close to, was a spy?

Seeing his panic, Mei Ling pressed on, her voice laced with desperation. "Jim, please. I can't do this alone. They'll expose me, and you'll be implicated, too. They have leverage over me, but they don't have anything over you. Yet."

The weight of her words threatened to suffocate him. He was trapped, caught in the crossfire of a foreign power struggle. Driven by fear and a twisted sense of protecting her, Morrison agreed to her demands.

Thus began a new phase in their twisted relationship. Mei Ling, no longer just the seductive aide, became his handler. She subtly manipulated his decisions, using their newfound intimacy as leverage. She planted seeds of doubt about his colleagues through her kisses, highlighting their shortcomings and fueling his disillusionment with the political landscape.

One day, she introduced him to Senator Robbins, a seemingly distinguished politician with a hidden agenda. Under the guise of political debate, Robbins tacitly set up Morrison in front of an audience not concerned so much about their constituencies but the interests of China.

The more Morrison burrowed into the subterranean den, the more he was going to blur the line between loyalty and betrayal. The idealistic congressman was morphing into a cog that was being manipulated with fear and a misguided effort to "protect" this woman who had become his most deadly secret.

Chapter Twelve:
Capitol's Hidden Truth

Senator Robbins. A man with a snake's tongue wrapped in polished silver welcomed Morrison with a strong handshake and a pretentious smile. "Congressman," he said, his voice filled with fake honey. "I hear very good things about you. Your dedication and discretion are highly praised by Mei Ling."

Morrison, torn between newfound loyalty to Mei Ling and a nagging sense of unease, simply nodded in acknowledgment. Robbins led him through a backroom as dimly illuminated as the Senator's front-facing office was amply appointed. Seated around a mahogany table, the faces of a group of individuals were cloaked in near-shadow.

"These are my esteemed colleagues." Robbins introduced them vaguely, their handshakes strong and their eyes beyond the range of expression. After all, had been introduced, Robbins cleared his throat and laid out an agenda.

"We are above the line of standard politics," he explained in a low voice as though they were having a conspiratorial conversation. "We think that true progress is born from being bold enough to act, even if it's by making exceptions to the established norms."

Morrison became increasingly uneasy, feeling somehow that there was wrongness in all this veiled language. The two groups penetrated deeply, one into the other's association, and it was utterly clear that they, to some seeming good within the group and calling themselves "Hydra," would manipulate not only legislation and policy but even also intelligence for their own purposes. Specifics eluded him, although, intuitionally again, Morrison felt that whatever their final goal might be, it was suspiciously in harmony with those of China.

Weeks turned into days, and Morrison's worry became a fear. The more hours he put in with Robbins, the more reasons he found not to trust the senator.

One fateful night, after ending a session early, Morrison saw a sight that confirmed his worst beliefs.

Over by an alley, standing across the street, was Senator Robbins in a huddle with someone whose features were covered by a fedora. The latter spoke to him in a language that Morrison could not understand, but from the grave look and the furtive glances they exchanged with each other, nothing could be clearer: it was foreign intelligence, MSS.

Morrison broke into a cold sweat and felt nauseous all of a sudden. The senator he had started to trust, the man who had been his confidante within the ranks, was a double agent, playing for both sides for his own benefit. The truth came like a light bolt, shattering the delicate trust he had managed to build within Hydra.

Meanwhile, within the dimly lit backroom, Robbins, oblivious to Morrison's discovery, concluded his meeting with a satisfied smirk. He had witnessed Morrison's discomfort with their recent operations, interpreting it as a sign of weakness. He saw in Morrison an opportunity to solidify his own position within the group, a potential ally who could be easily manipulated.

"Congressman Morrison," Robbins announced upon returning, his voice laced with a hint of triumph, "I believe you have the potential to make a significant contribution to our cause."

Morrison could only nod, his mind reeling from the exposure. He was trapped in a web of his own weaving—caught by his loyalty to Mei Ling from falling off the tightrope between conscience and betrayal. The friend-foe and right-wrong lines were hopelessly and irretrievably blurred. The murky waters of espionage needed to be waded through with a heavy heart and a gnawing sense of dread.

Senator Robbins, his eyes glinting with a predatory gleam, leaned closer to Morrison.

"We have a crucial task for you, Congressman," he stated, his voice low and measured. "A task that will require your unique skillset and discretion."

His stomach had done a double lutz. He knew, it was the moment of truth—a place from which there could be no coming back. Still, the grip of fear and his twisted sense of loyalty to Mei Ling silenced his internal protests. "What do you need me to do?" he asked, barely above a whisper.

"We need certain classified documents," Robbins cut in, undeterred as his eyes held Morrison, "from a high-security government facility. Your access to this system and familiarity with it will be greatly welcomed on this mission."

Morrison's mind raced. He crossed a line he never thought, he would—a blatant betrayal of his own oath to uphold the law and protect national security. But the vision that flashed through his mind was that of Mei Ling, her tears in her eyes imploring him to heed her plea. He knew only too well the dire consequences of his refusal to heed her voice.

He had agreed with great reluctance and had been mainly driven by an insidious amalgam of ambition, fear, and misguided loyalty, or maybe love. In the coming days, Robbins was to hold sessions in which, he briefed Morrison critically on each detail associated with his mission, making full use of his closeness and familiarity with security procedures. The Congressman, proud of being the greatest paragon of honesty, now fell into the hands of political scoundrels.

Under the cover of darkness, Morrison entered the compound, his heart pounding inside his chest with every careful step that he took. He wandered in those passageways, a virtual labyrinth, a stage for his mind—one constantly at war with the pull of his emotions; guilt yanked him back, and yet desperation and the prospect of life entwined with Mei Ling wanted him forward.

He successfully breached the secure server room and retrieved the designated files, his hands shaking as he transferred them to a hidden device. Escaping the facility felt like a scene from a spy thriller, a stark contrast to the life he had known before.

Returning to the underbelly, Morrison presented the documents to Robbins, a sense of accomplishment warring with the growing turmoil within him. Robbins accepted the files with a satisfied smirk, his eyes conveying an ominous sense of power.

"Welcome to the fold, Congressman," he declared, his voice laced with a hint of victory. "You have proven yourself a valuable asset. Your contributions will be instrumental in achieving our goals."

As Morrison left the room, the weight of his actions settled on him like a suffocating blanket. He had crossed the line twice, venturing into a world of shadows and deceit.

The idealistic Congressman was gone, replaced by a man who unknowingly participated in covert operations that threatened the very nation he had sworn to serve. The line between his true loyalty and the manipulative control of Hydra had become dangerously blurred, leaving him trapped in a perilous game of deception with no easy escape.

****

The tension in the room crackled like static electricity as Mei Ling scrolled through Congressman Morrison's files. Her eyes locked onto a document titled "Project Horizon," and a jolt of recognition shot through her. Though heavily classified, the mention of AI-powered robotic soldiers sent chills down her spine.

"This is the moment that I was waiting for," she murmured, the weight of the information pressing down on her. This was the key— the game-changer China craved to tip the global balance of power in their favor.

Torn between her loyalty to her homeland and the unexpected affection that had bloomed for Morrison, a war raged within her.

Could she betray everything she was raised to believe in—everything she'd sacrificed for—to protect this man?

Taking a deep breath, she activated her secure communication device hidden within a desk drawer. Her voice, a mere whisper laced with urgency, crackled through the speaker. "Dragon, it's me, dragonfly. I need to talk to you. Now."

Static filled the line for a beat before Dragon's voice, a mixture of concern and excitement, filled her ear. "Dragonfly, report. What's going on?"

"I found something," she began, briefly explaining the Project Horizon document and its potential significance. "It's crucial we get this information to our superiors. But I'm worried. Security around the project has tightened, and I..." her voice trailed off, the fear of exposure settling in her stomach.

"We understand the risks," Dragon replied, his voice firm yet laced with empathy. "But this is critical intelligence. We'll work on extracting you as soon as possible. Stay safe, Dragonfly."

Heeding the dragon's instructions, Mei Ling continued her charade. The once-discreet meetings with her handlers became more frequent, their demands growing increasingly insistent. Their harsh voices contrasted sharply with Morrison's gentle inquiries about her late nights and secretive phone calls.

"Is everything alright, Mei Ling?" Morrison asked one evening, his brow furrowed with concern as he watched her pack her bag.

"Just some late-night reports as usual," she replied with a forced smile, her heart pounding against her ribs. The lie felt heavy on her tongue, but it was the only shield she had left.

The facade began to crumble, when news reached her of an upcoming security sweep at work. Her access logs, flagged for suspicious activity, confirmed her worst fears. She felt the walls closing in and the noose of her destiny getting tighter day by day.

One night, Morrison slept peacefully, and Mei Ling made her decision. Her loyalty to her country, her training, and everything that she lived for was in terrible conflict with the love and affection that she kept for the man lying beside her. It was indeed with a very heavy heart that Mei Ling knew she had to make a choice.

"Forgive me, Jim," she whispered while touching the shoulder of his sleeping form before padding out of the room. Tucking a single tear-stained note under a book on the table, she silently let herself out into the night, her decision weighing upon her like an old cloak sewn of lead.

Calling upon every skill honed by years of clandestine operations, she eluded security, and slipped out of the country. Reuniting with her network in China, Mei Ling was hollowed out by her feelings of accomplishment. The mission was complete, the information secured, but at an unbearable personal cost.

All those years of building a life filled with nurturing love became shattered fragments of what was and would never be. The weight of her choices, the betrayal she had committed, and the love she had to sacrifice were her constant companions. Her footsteps led her forward into a new chapter, with her future forever remaining shrouded in uncertainty, haunted by the ghosts of the past and the might-consequence-double game in which she had played.

On the plane, she looked down at the city teeming with life, and her heart twinge briefly for the life she'd left behind. The man, she tried to love—the life they could have had together—shattered into tiny pieces of glass that she could never return to.

"Welcome back, Dragonfly," her handler said with a voice barely holding any warmth. But before she could answer, a gunshot was heard, and Mei Ling was silenced forever.

***

Brett adjusted the weight of the worn backpack slung over his shoulder as he stood under the imposing shadow of the Capitol building. Moonlight cast long, spectral fingers across the facade, momentarily transforming the monument into a silent sentinel guarding secrets within its walls.

Tonight, Brett was determined to wrest those secrets free.

Months had passed since his last foray into the hidden chambers beneath the Capitol, a harrowing near-miss with security that still sent shivers down his spine. But the fire in his gut—the desire to expose the truth that festered in the heart of American democracy—burned brighter than ever.

Taking a deep breath, Brett slipped into a side entrance, his movements practiced and silent. The familiar musty air of the building greeted him—a blend of old paper with dust and a faint odor of long-forgotten dreams. He made his way along the corridors; the narrow beams of the flashlight guided his walk, and dreadfully, every click-clack of his shoes sounded clear through silence.

He reached his destination, a hidden doorway concealed behind a portrait of a romanticized scene of the Founding Fathers, and Brett paused. The rapid rhythm of his heart pounding against his ribs sent adrenaline rushing through him as he gripped the cold metal door handle with the weight of the unknown pressing down on him.

"Nothing else to do now but to go forward," he whispered, though his own words were again absolutely senseless among the infinite silence.

With a deep breath, he pressed more with his hand to make the door creak open wider. All that was able to be seen inside was nothing but a dark room—the sharp darkness that was in contrast to the moonlight that filtered inside from the door that never existed from where he had come.

Brett took another deep breath and flicked his flashlight on; its beam cut through the gloom to catch the outlines of a cavernous place, dusty, and lined with towering cabinets. The weight of time hung heavily in the air, thick and heavy, and his breath rasped out in the silence that surrounded him. "This is it," he said, his voice low and reverent. "This is, where the truth is hidden."

He crept carefully forward his boots agitating dust motes that pirouetted among the beams of the flashlight. Each creak of the floorboards sent a quaking tremor of anticipation through him. He scanned the rows of cabinets with files that seemed to have aged; the labels were mostly faded and illegible.

"Monroe," he rasped as his fingers ran over the yellowed lettering of one such folder.

His heart missed a beat. Senator Monroe—the figure from whispers and hushed rumors—the one who stammered onto something big, something that got him 'silenced' under suspicious circumstances. Is this the clue? This is the key to the maze of deception that held the country's heart.

His fingers trembled as he took a firm hold of it and extracted the folder, keeping the worn leather cool and dry against his skin. He flipped it open, breath catching in his throat at the stark black file insignia emblazoned on the inside cover. "Black File." Only submitted for the most sensitive and damning pieces of information.

"Monroe was really on to something big," Brett murmured, his voice filled with a mixture of awe and trepidation.

Opening the file, his eyes scanned across it and went wide. Foreign, or just plain domestic, dignitaries it held—US Senators, Congressmen. Dates, figures, and places are all meticulously recorded, along with sums for tender and damning details of dirty deals, payoffs, and bribes. The volume alone was mind-numbing—the face of the great, big corruption web that ran throughout the highest circles of power.

"This isn't real," he murmured, the sound of his voice seeming a little louder than the beat of his heart. "It's larger than anything anyone has ever thought about."

Sweat broke out on his forehead, and it had nothing to do with the physical exertion. Pandora's box had fallen upon his head, and now it's very secrets jeopardized the very nation he believed in.

"I have to get this out of here," he thought, his mind racing. "I have to expose this to the public. But how?"

He knew the risks were immense. But the thought of turning back, of allowing this web of corruption to continue to flourish, filled him with a sense of dread even greater than the fear of the unknown consequences.

"I can't do anything," he said, his voice firm with resolve. "The truth needs to be out there, no matter the cost."

With a newfound determination, Brett began meticulously copying the incriminating documents. He knew, this was just the beginning, but tonight, in the heart of the silent Capitol building, he had taken the first step towards exposing a darkness that threatened to engulf the nation.

Chapter Thirteen:
Realization Of A Conspiracy: Potus's Involvement

Brett's heart hammered against his ribs as his eyes snagged on a name scrawled across a page in the black file: POTUS. The President of the United States? His breath caught in his throat.

"The President?" he breathed, disbelief lacing his voice. This was a whole other ballgame. This was bigger than anything he'd ever imagined.

He flipped through the pages frantically, searching for any mention of the president, or any clue as to what this special file might contain. Finally, a glimmer of hope—a small note tucked into a pocket at the back—mentioned a specific cabinet, one not marked with any label.

A thrill of determination surged through him. "The POTUS file is in that cabinet," he whispered, more to himself than anyone else. "I gotta see what's in there."

Brett hurried across the room with a newfound urgency and yanked open the unmarked cabinet door. Inside, nestled amongst innocuous folders, lay a file emblazoned with the presidential seal. This was it. The key.

His hands trembled slightly as he retrieved the file, the black file clutched tightly under his other arm. He knew that he couldn't waste any time.

Back at his residence, Brett worked with a focused intensity. He meticulously scanned each page of both files, the hum of the machine a steady counterpoint to the pounding in his chest. Every detail, every scrap of information, had to be preserved. Finally, with a sigh of relief, he ejected the thumb drive, a digital copy of his explosive findings safely stored.

One last sweep of his eyes across the computer screen confirmed everything had transferred correctly. Now, it was time to assemble the team. He grabbed his phone, his finger hovering over a familiar number.

"Get everyone to headquarters, now," he barked into the receiver, his voice tight with urgency. "We've got a situation. A big one. And I need all hands on deck to figure out what our next move is."

He hung up, his pulse still racing. He knew the weight of what he held in his hands. This was bigger than any of them could have ever imagined, and the fate of something much larger than himself now rested on their shoulders.

***

The metallic groan of the Nexus headquarters door echoed through the sterile briefing room as Brett hurried in, a whirlwind of urgency. His eyes darted around the room, landing on the assembled task force: Agent Henderson, a stoic man with a gaze as sharp as a tack; Agent Carter, the ever-skeptical tech whiz; and the rest of their hand-picked team.

Without a preamble, Brett slammed two files onto the expansive table in the center of the room. The sharp crack of leather against laminate sent a jolt through the team, instantly pulling them to attention.

"Alright, people," Brett began, his voice tight with barely suppressed excitement. "Fasten your seatbelts. We hit the jackpot."

Agent Henderson, ever the picture of composure, raised an eyebrow. "Care to elaborate, Brett? You look like, you just unearthed a UFO."

A humorless chuckle escaped Brett's lips. "Not quite, Henderson, but close. This is bigger. This changes everything." He gestured toward the black file. "This," he continued, his voice hushed, "is a black file. Names, dates, and enough incriminating evidence to sink a battleship. Foreign dignitaries, U.S. Senators, fattened by the stench of corruption, all neatly documented."

A collective gasp rippled through the room. Usually glued to his laptop screen, Agent Carter leaned back in his chair, eyes wide. "Holy," he breathed, the rest of the sentence hanging heavy in the air.

Ignoring the murmurs, Brett flipped open the second file, the presidential seal glinting accusingly under the harsh white lights.

"And this," he declared, his voice laced with a grim determination, "is the POTUS file."

The room exploded. Agent Smith, a seasoned investigator known for his unflappable demeanor, slammed his fist on the table. "The President? Are you out of your mind, Brett?"

Brett met his gaze head-on. "I have never been more sure of anything in my life, Smith. This is real. This is deep."

The silence descended once more, thick, and heavy. Brett's revelation settled on the team like a shroud. They exchanged nervous glances, the gravity of the situation sinking in.

With a deep breath, Brett gestured towards the nearby computer station. Ever the pragmatist, Agent Carter sprang into action, plugging in the thumb drive containing the digitized files. A low hum filled the room as the data was transferred.

A complex web of information began to take shape on the massive screen that dominated one wall. Lines connected names, dates flickered into view, and a horrifying picture of widespread corruption started to emerge. The team leaned closer, their faces grim, as they absorbed the damning evidence.

The room buzzed with nervous energy as the task force scrutinized the newly integrated documents. Lines and arrows, representing the flow of information, snaked across the massive screen, weaving a tangled web of corruption that seemed to have its origin point right in the Oval Office.

"This is it, folks," Agent Henderson declared, his voice tight with a mixture of excitement and trepidation. "These new files are a gold mine. They are proof positive that could bring the entire house of cards tumbling down on the President."

Agent Carter whistled, a low, drawn-out sound that echoed in the sterile room. "Look at these communication logs," he said, his finger tracing a series of encrypted messages. "Fake names, burner phones, the whole clandestine nine yards. They knew what they were doing was wrong, and they went to great lengths to hide it."

Special Agent Ramirez, never one to shirk at the fastidious, settled back in his chair, eyes locked onto the screen. "That's a violation of every kind of protocol I know," he grumbled under his breath. "They were careful. Yes, they were careful. But this," he glanced back at the screen with more interest, "leads somewhere else, deeper. We're so close, I swear."

A heavy silence descended upon the room as the gravity of the situation settled in. Special Agent Sarah Smith, her expression a mask of concern, spoke first. "We need to tread carefully, Brett. This is explosive information. A single misstep could blow the whole operation sky high."

Brett nodded curtly, his jaw clenched tight. "I understand, Sarah. That's why, I've already encrypted copies of the entire data set. Our next move is two-fold: verification and investigation." He gestured toward the black file. "We need to confirm the authenticity of these documents; make sure they're not some elaborate forgery."

"And what about Senator Monroe?" Agent Smith inquired, her brow furrowed. "These communications seem to point towards some level of involvement on his part. Digging deeper could lead us straight to his doorstep."

A steely glint hardened Brett's eyes. "We can't run from the truth, Smith. Whatever that rabbit hole leads to, it's our job to find out. In the darkness, some people thrive on corruption. It's our job to drag it and throw it out into the light, maybe even expose it for what it truly is."

All task force members nodded determinedly in a wave. They could not help but realize the enormity of their task. They were on the verge of stumbling into a conspiracy that stretched to the top, possibly uncovering truths that could shatter any semblance of national trust. The once serene underground chamber beneath the Capitol—where secret sessions had long furtively taken place and for which it had become notorious—had now turned into a veritable war room. Still, for the kind of battle none of them could ever have dreamt of.

*****

The harsh white lights of the interrogation room threw a sterilized light at the young man sitting across from Brett. Of Congressman Morrison's staff, David Davis looked, if possible, even less beyond his twenties, wilting like a flower under the frequent glare. The confident swagger he usually displayed in Morrison's shadow had evaporated, replaced by a tremor that ran through his body with each flickering light.

"Mr. Davis," Brett began, his voice devoid of emotion, "we've been taking a closer look at your financial activities lately. Let's just say the picture they paint is rather concerning."

David swallowed hard, the sound echoing unnaturally in the silent room. His gaze darted around, searching for an escape route that didn't exist. "I, uh, I don't know what you're talking about," he stammered, his voice barely a whisper.

Brett leaned forward with a predatory glint in his eyes. He placed a thick stack of bank statements on the metal table with a dramatic flourish. "These, Mr. Davis," he said, tapping the documents with a resounding thud, "are records of significant transfers to offshore accounts. Accounts that, coincidentally, align perfectly with your recent trips abroad. Trips, I might add that was curiously absent from your official travel logs."

David's face was drained of color. The confident facade he'd so carefully constructed crumbled like a sandcastle under a tidal wave. Panic replaced the bravado, his eyes wide with a desperate plea for mercy.

"I don't," he stammered, his voice cracking. I was just trying to help my family," he exclaimed, clutching at the first straw he could grasp.

A humorless scoff escaped Brett's lips. "Is that what you call it, Mr. Davis?" he countered, his voice hardening. "Selling classified information to a foreign power, an enemy of our nation, qualifies as 'helping your family'?"

David slumped forward, defeated. The carefully constructed dam holding back his guilt finally burst. Tears welled up in his eyes, spilling over onto his pale cheeks.

"I never meant for it to go this far," he confessed, his voice choked with emotion. "It started small; I just overheard a few details here and there. But then... the money. They kept offering more, and I was stupid. I couldn't resist the temptation."

Words flooded from him, one after another in rapid succession, trying to offload the pressure on his conscience. He spoke of meetings in the blackest backstreets and shared whispered telephone calls in the dead of night that sounded like harmless greetings but were insidious messages. It puts a dewy covering over everything that Morrison himself is. A web of deceit is being spun literally from the man at the center: Congressman Morrison, a pseudo-squeaky clean politician using his office to benefit himself and for monetary greed.

With Davis's tearful confession captured on video and securely locked away, Brett didn't waste a single second. He barked orders into his headset, his voice crackling with a mix of urgency and satisfaction: "Alright, team, listen up! We've got a live one. Move in, secure Davis's apartment and seize all his digital assets—laptops, phones, hard drives—the whole nine yards. We need every scrap of data he has."

Moments later, a flurry of activity erupted within Nexus headquarters. Members of the task force, clad in tactical gear, sprang into action. Agent Carter, the tech whiz, practically vibrated with excitement. "Finally! A chance to get my hands on some real intel," he muttered, grabbing his digital forensics toolkit.

Meanwhile, back in the interrogation room, Brett kept a watchful eye on Davis, who now resembled a deflated balloon, all the air of arrogance sucked out of him. "Alright, Davis," Brett said, his voice calm but firm, "you've come clean about the information leaks. Now, let's talk about the money trail. How did Morrison funnel his ill-gotten gains?"

Davis sniffled, wiping his nose with a crumpled tissue. "He was very careful. Offshore accounts in the Cayman Islands were shell companies with names nobody could trace. He had everything set up perfectly."

"And what about his lifestyle?" Brett pressed. "All those fancy cars you mentioned, the luxury condo downtown—how did he explain those away?"

A flicker of bitterness crossed Davis's face. "He said, they were 'family investments.' He said, his wife had a knack for picking winners on the stock market. I laughed about it the whole time."

As the conversation continued, Davis spilled more and more details. He spoke of hidden compartments in Morrison's office furniture, coded messages disguised as grocery lists, and secret meetings under darkness. Each revelation was another brick in the wall of evidence against the seemingly untouchable Congressman.

By the end of the day, the task force had a mountain of damning data. The financial records of Davis showed a shadowy web of lies, while his testimony painted an incredibly damning picture of Morrison's greed and betrayal. It seems that for every dignified politician, this one is now a traitor, able to sell his country just for a taste of the high life. There was no let-up in the flutter, but the struggle for justice had already just begun. The noose was gradual, minute by minute, drawing around Morrison's neck. All that was being unraveled was undeserved corruption and the imminent birth of a truth that would be unpalatable to all.

***

Congressman Morrison sat in the station's interrogation room, cruelly flickering fluorescent lights from above casting hard, shadowy circles across his sweating forehead. His face, ordinarily down-at-the-heels but well-kept, showed a mask of self-control that had been cracked under the last load of evidence. David Davis' confession had ripped the curtain back, exposing the ugly truth of Morrison's betrayal.

Across the table, Brett leaned forward, his eyes narrowing. "Checkmate, Congressman," he declared, his voice devoid of warmth. "We have Davis's complete testimony, your financial records—a veritable treasure trove of incriminating transactions—and enough corroborating evidence to bury you deeper than a Mariana Trench shrimp."

Morrison sputtered, a desperate flicker of defiance warring with the rising tide of fear in his eyes. "This is... this is a witch hunt! You can't do this to me! I've served this country with honor for decades."

Brett snorted a humorless sound that echoed in the sterile room. "Served? Or soiled, Congressman? Selling classified secrets to the Chinese for a hefty personal bonus? That's your definition of honorable service?"

He slammed a thick file onto the table, the sharp crack echoing in the tense silence. Documents spilled out, a visual representation of Morrison's elaborate web of deceit—offshore accounts with names that wouldn't fool a toddler, coded messages disguised as grocery lists, a meticulous record of his clandestine dealings with the Chinese. Each piece of evidence was a shard of truth, piercing the carefully constructed illusion he'd built for years.

The facade crumbled completely. Morrison felt like a wave of weariness surged through him unexpectedly, stunning his shoulders momentarily. All the bluster and bravado seemed to drain from him in a rush, like a hole in a bucket spilling water. "I did what I had to do for my country," he huskily stammered.

He countered in a hard-sounding voice. "Spare me the sob story, Congressman. It wasn't about the country. This was about greed. You had ambition, which ran through you so fast that you didn't see anything else. You had your oath, your country, and."

Morrison's eyes ran about the room; he must have been looking for a non-existent escape route. He opened his mouth to protest, but then thought better of it. The words simply could not hold; no, it was not right. He looked more like a cornered animal trapped in a cage of his own making.

One bead of sweat traced a slow path from the congressman's temple, almost impossible to miss, given the light's stare. All bluster leavened with a raw vulnerability that could easily twist at a corner of Brett's empathy. Grasping his opportunity, he took a step back, a calculated shift in posture.

"Now, Morrison, here's the deal then," Brett said, his voice as soft as before but with no less firmness. "The option is yours."

Morrison's head snapped upright, and there, for just a moment, a flicker of something danced in his bloodshot eyes. "What... what do you want from me?" he managed hoarsely.

"The truth, Congressman," Brett replied, his gaze unwavering. "The whole, unvarnished truth. And most importantly, who else is swimming in this cesspool with you?"

Morrison hesitated, his gaze darting around the sterile room like a trapped animal seeking an escape hatch. He knew that the jig was up, but the prospect of dragging others down with him offered a sliver of twisted satisfaction.

"Robbins," he finally croaked, the name tumbling out like a confession. "Senator... Senator Robbins. He's the one who orchestrated this whole damn thing. Used me like a puppet, dangling information and bribes in front of me."

Brett felt a jolt course through him. This was bigger than he'd ever imagined. A single corrupt Congressman was bad enough, but a powerful Senator with his fingers wrapped around the gears of Washington? This changes everything.

"Robbins, huh?" Brett repeated, his voice laced with a dangerous calm. "Tell me everything. How did he recruit you? What threats did he use? Who else is involved?"

Morrison launched into a desperate plea, pouring out a torrent of accusations. He described how Robbins had approached him years ago, dangling the promise of political favors, and lucrative opportunities in exchange for classified information. He spoke of veiled threats against his family, a chilling reminder that his compliance wasn't a choice but a forced surrender.

With each revelation, the picture became clearer. Senator Robbins wasn't just another name on a list; if the use of the word "blackmail" had any significance, it was an inside power that was controlling it like a puppeteer pulling the strings from the shadows. The implication of knowing what he knew dragged down Brett's shoulders as if there was a leaden cloak on them. He wasn't spilling the beans on one dirty politician anymore—he was staring a viper's nest of deceit right in the eyes, which coiled and coiled to the very heart of the political establishment.

Chapter Fourteen:
Morrison's Downfall

The chilling silence that followed Senator Robbins's revelation appeared to hang in the room as if some dark specter had just swept through. It wasn't just the Congressman himself; there was a vast, taut web of corruption reaching up into prestigious places in the power tower. And maybe seeing the opportunity to rip that network of corruption apart, Brett took the very cold, calculating risk.

"Morrison," I breathed hoarsely, controlling all the rage within me to speak in a very soft voice, "you're in a very delicate position. Evidence against you is substantive; penalties for your actions are severe."

Morrison's face was drained of color. The flicker of hope that had ignited moments ago dimmed considerably. He swallowed hard, the sound echoing unnaturally in the silent room.

"But," Brett continued, leaning forward, "there might be a way out. A chance to redeem yourself, to some extent."

Morrison's eyes darted back up, a glimmer of desperate curiosity replacing the resignation. "What... what are you talking about?" he croaked.

"A full confession," Brett declared, his voice firm. "You cooperate fully; tell us everything you know about Senator Robbins' involvement, and in exchange, I'll advocate for leniency in your sentencing."

The offer hung in the air, a lifeline thrown across a churning sea of legal repercussions. Morrison's mind raced with the consequences of both choices swirling in a dizzying vortex.

"Leniency? You mean... no jail time?" He stammered, the words tumbling out in a rush.

"The possibility exists," Brett replied coolly, "but it depends entirely on the value of your information. If your testimony leads to a successful prosecution of Senator Robbins, then leniency becomes a much more realistic option."

Finally, with a heavy sigh that seemed to carry the burden of his choices, he spoke.

"Alright," he conceded, lacing his voice. "I'll do it. I'll tell you everything that I know about Senator Robbins."

A satisfied glint flickered in Brett's eyes. That was only a teaser, of course. In the course of trying to dig up just one corrupt politician, it would eventually stumble onto something far, far worse—that, a secret galaxy of power known only by its code name—Hydra, whose many heads burrowed out through the government itself.

While the slaughter and the feasting went on in parts of the town, behind other walls of the place, a burning drama was continuing in the Oval Office. Senator Robbins paced back and forth on the heavy carpet, his face pallid and sweating as if he had bled white. His heart hammered against his ribs like a trapped bird, little shooting pains of fear spiking. The President, once the Senator's confidant, packed behind his resolute desk with that expression of his, which might as well have been cast in stone.

"Mr. President," Robbins blurted out, his voice cracking under the pressure, "we need to talk. This investigation... they're closing in. We're both in this together, remember?"

He approached the desk, his posture a mixture of desperation and defiance. "The network, the shell companies—we used them both. We can't let them expose us!"

His words hung heavy in the air, a desperate plea for the president's support. The "network" he referred to was a complex maze of financial secrecy, the lifeblood of their illicit activities. It masked their true dealings, allowing them to siphon off millions for their own gain.

"Hydra," Robbins continued, his voice dropping to a conspiratorial whisper, reminding the president of the clandestine group that held the reins of power, manipulating the world from the shadows.

But the president's reaction was far from what Robbins had anticipated. The warmth and camaraderie of their past meetings were gone, replaced by a chilling indifference. The president leaned back in his chair, steeping his fingers, and a single, icy question pierced the tense silence.

"And what exactly makes you think that I want your help, Senator?"

Senator Robbins' blood ran cold. The warmth in the Oval Office seemed to leach away entirely, replaced by a glacial atmosphere that sent shivers down his spine. The president, once a jovial colleague, now looked like a predator, eyeing wounded prey.

"Every man for himself, Senator," came the president's reply, his tone quiet but equally unforgiving. "Or a little more. Heed when covering your tracks next time wouldn't be such a bad idea."

Robbins's mind reeled. The man whom he perceived to be one of his closest and most trusted confidants, a co-conspirator of sorts, now cast him to the wind. Panic tore at his throat, cold dread slithering down his spine.

"But... but the network, the shell companies," It finally hit him; the newfound desperation just made it more evident in his voice. "We are a team together, Mr. President—you can't let me down now!"

A cruel smile fell broad across the president's lips, turning the corners up in the barest caricature of chumminess. "Oh, Senator," he hissed, "you've got things just a little bit wrong. I've hidden my tracks quite well. You, on the other hand, let the sentence trail off, meaning it was heavy in the air.

"You have nothing on me," Robbins shot back, bravado uttered in a simple act to claw back a piece of control. But even his own ears couldn't mask the hollow ring of his words. The president held all the cards, and Robbins knew it.

"Try to expose me, Senator," the President continued, his voice low and menacing, "and I will make you regret the day you were born. My resources are vast, and my reach extends far beyond your comprehension. Consider yourself be warned."

The weight of the president's threat settled on Robbins like a leaden shroud. He knew the man wasn't bluffing. The ruthless politician who now sat across from him was a far cry from the charming leader he'd once known. Despair threatened to consume him, with the walls of his carefully constructed world closing in.

But as he turned to leave the Oval Office, the dim flickering of a grudge against the man who had betrayed him. He wasn't going down without a fight. He knew the president's secrets—the skeletons hidden in his meticulously guarded closet. And those secrets, he realized, were his weapons.

"You may hold all the power now, Mr. President," Robbins said, his voice surprisingly steady, "but power is a fickle mistress. The truth has a way of coming out, no matter how deeply you bury it. Our people need to know the truth about all this rottenness right from the very core of this government, about the evil, sinister forces hidden in the shadows, controlling from behind."

A flicker of surprise crossed the president's face, quickly replaced by a steely glint in his eyes. "A bold statement, Senator," he countered. "But are you prepared to face the consequences of your actions? You may bring me down, but your own destruction is guaranteed."

Robbins squared his shoulders, and across his features, a new resolve seemed to harden. "Then, I may go down," he said, more conviction coming into his voice, "but I won't go down alone. I'll shine a light on that thing. Expose your little cabal; your half-century of secrecy is about to become nothing but a memory! The fight might just be starting on this."

Senator Robbins ushered a final glance over at the president with as much defiance as he could haughtily muster. On that look, he spun on a swivel of spit-polished shoe leather and barreled upon the crowd of great men of power and influence in their own chamber. The divides were set, and a betrayed lone wolf had reached over them, now becoming a warrior for truth against the very system he had once embraced. A fight to save the nation's soul had erupted, and its tremors would be heard worldwide.

***

The news that Senator Robbins was part of the espionage ring was like a political bomb. Shockwaves pierced the highest corridors of power, utter disregard for decades of his careful image. The once-respected Senator was now a pariah, his name synonymous with betrayal.

Meanwhile, the task force, fueled by a relentless pursuit of justice, worked around the clock. Brett, his eyes red from long nights, spearheaded the evidence gathering. David Davis's testimony, gushing with emotion and the tale of secret meetings and under-the-table dealings, was priceless. With every word, a new nail in the coffin of treachery by Morrison and Robbins was driven.

The day finally arrived when Brett had to square up to Senator Robbins. He rang the doorbell of the Senator's luxurious mansion, and for some reason, it seemed to him as if it towered to the very height of the thunderclouds above it. The wind howled like a banshee, rain lashing against the bulletproof windows of the study. It mirrored the tempestuous turmoil within Brett as he ascended the steps.

A tense calm reigned within; there was no other way to put it, nothing less than a stark contrast to the storm outside. Subdued by the atmosphere, the luxurious furniture almost gleamed in the soft lamplight, their mahogany walls lined with leather-bound books— suffocated by treachery and the certain admission of guilt.

Senator Robbins turned out to be smoothed, but still, he was a great gradation downward from the others. With his face ashen and damp with sweat, he leaned forward. The walls of denial he'd constructed with bluster and political maneuvering had crumbled under the relentless assault of evidence and Davis's scorching testimony.

"Senator Robbins," Brett began, his voice low and steely, "the jig is officially up. We have enough to bury you and your little operation deeper than the Mariana Trench."

Robbins flinched at the harsh words, his gaze darting around the room like a trapped animal seeking an escape that wasn't there. "I... I don't know what you're talking about," he stammered, his voice husky. But the tremor in his voice betrayed his bravado.

Brett slammed a file on the table, the sharp crack echoing in the tense silence. It contained transcripts of intercepted communications, financial records detailing suspicious transfers, and documented meetings with known Chinese agents. The evidence was irrefutable.

"This evidence," Brett continued his gaze unwavering, "points directly to your involvement in espionage. You and Congressman Morrison sold classified information to the Chinese for a hefty sum. Now, I have one question, Senator."

He leaned forward, his voice dropping to a low growl. "Where is the AI program?"

Robbins's eyes widened in a flicker of surprise. The AI program—a vital piece of national security research—wasn't mentioned in any evidence they'd presented. How did Brett know about it?

"W-what AI program?" he stammered, the facade of composure finally fracturing.

Robbins swallowed hard, the sound a dry rasp in the tense silence of the opulent study. His face, drained of color, seemed years older under the harsh lamplight. "I..." he stammered, his voice barely a whisper. "I took it."

Brett's eyes narrowed. "The AI program," he confirmed, his voice a low growl. "You stole it from the Horizon facility, didn't you?"

Robbins's head bobbed once in a weak affirmative. "Yeah, but I haven't. It's still here."

A beat of tense silence followed, punctuated only by the rhythmic drumming of rain against the bulletproof windows. The air crackled with a dangerous energy, the threat of violence hanging heavy in the room.

Finally, Brett leaned forward, his posture predatory. "Then give it up, Senator," he commanded, his voice a steely rasp. "Now."

Robbins flinched under Brett's intensity, his eyes darting around the room like a trapped animal seeking an escape route. "I... I will," he stammered, the veneer of defiance finally crumbling. "But you... you have to understand the pressure that I was under."

"Spare me the sob story, Senator," Brett countered, his voice devoid of sympathy. "You betrayed your country for personal gain. Now, are you going to cooperate or not?"

Robbins hesitated, a flickering of desperation on his face. "Look," he blurted out, his voice ragged, "if I'm helping you recover the program, is there any chance of leniency?"

Brett studied him for a long moment, his expression unreadable. "If you cooperate fully," he finally conceded, his voice laced with steel, "and help us get the program back in the right hands, then I'll do everything I can to put in a good word for you. But that depends entirely on your level of good faith."

A glimmer of hope flickered in Robbins's eyes. He took a deep, shaky breath. "Alright," he agreed, his voice hoarse. "I'll show you where it is."

He rose unsteadily from his plush armchair, his movements stiff and robotic. With a defeated sigh, he walked over to a seemingly unremarkable bookcase, his back to Brett. Reaching behind a row of leather-bound classics, he plucked a small, innocuous bronze figurine from the shelf. His hands trembled as he placed it on his desk, and then he traced the outline of a hidden latch with his shaking finger.

With a soft push and click, a hidden compartment at its base gave way to a palm-sized device bathed in an ebbing, pulsating glow of blue. It gave off an audible hum as if it were something solid, with the energy it harbored.

Shaking, Robbins fumbled in and plucked the burning device from its resting place. He presented it to Brett with both hands as if offering up a peace gift. "There." His voice was a hoarse rasp. "The AI program. Only one copy, I swear."

Brett remained still for a moment, his eyes fixed on the device. It was this little wonder of technology, humming with potential and secrets. It could very well, falling into the wrong hands, mean the release of an unstoppable army of some sort of robot, an all-too-powerful counterpart to Pandora's box of its day.

He reached out and took the device from Robbins, handling it with a reverence he hadn't expected, even to himself. "Thank you," he said gruffly, his voice surprisingly devoid of anger. "Show me where this army is."

Robbins's face went pale again, but he nodded. "Alright. Follow me." As they both walked to a bullet proof car in the parking lot.

***

As they arrived at Horizon Facility, Brett's grip tightened around the device. He followed Robbins through a series of secure hallways and down a flight of stairs into a hidden underground facility. The walls, lined with reinforced steel, whispered secrets kept from the world above. Finally, they stopped in front of a heavily guarded door.

Robbins keyed in a code, and the door slid open with a hydraulic hiss. Inside, the room buzzed with an eerie hum, illuminated by sterile blue light. In the center of the room stood several imposing figures—prototypes of the robotic soldiers. Brett's eyes widened at the sight.

Their exoskeleton gleamed under the harsh lights. Made from a composite of titanium alloy and carbon fiber; the frame looked both lightweight and incredibly durable. They stood about seven feet tall, with articulated joints that mimicked human movement with uncanny precision. The limbs, reinforced with hydraulic actuators, promised strength far beyond that of any human.

The chest plate housed a sophisticated array of sensors and a compact power unit designed to keep the soldiers operational for extended periods. The head featured an array of cameras and LIDAR (Light Detection and Ranging) systems, giving it 360-degree vision and advanced targeting capabilities. Every inch of the exoskeleton screamed efficiency and lethality.

Brett took a step closer, eyes narrowing as he took in the details. The hands were equipped with both fine motor controls for delicate tasks and retractable blades for combat scenarios. The legs, reinforced and spring-loaded, indicated an ability to jump great distances or sprint at high speeds.

"These soldiers," Robbins continued, "are designed for both combat and support roles. They can operate autonomously or be remotely controlled. The exoskeletons are equipped with adaptive camouflage, capable of blending into their surroundings. They're practically invisible to the naked eye and most surveillance systems."

Brett walked closer, inspecting the fine details of the design. He noted the intricate network of sensors and the sophisticated control modules embedded within the exoskeletons. "Impressive," he muttered, his earlier anger momentarily overshadowed by fascination.

Robbins, sensing a shift in Brett's demeanor, took a deep breath. "The AI program you're holding," he said, "is the key to controlling them. Without it, they're just advanced machinery. With it, they become a strategic asset—or a devastating threat."

Brett turned to face him, the gravity of the situation clear in his eyes. "Then we need to ensure this doesn't fall into the wrong hands. Show me how to shut it down."

Robbins nodded, moving towards a nearby console. "There's a kill switch," he explained, his fingers flying over the controls. "But it can only be activated with a specific biometric scan and passcode."

Brett watched intently as Robbins initiated the shutdown sequence. The hum of the exoskeletons slowly died down, their lights dimming until they stood inert and lifeless.

"Now," Brett said, his voice a low rumble, "let's make sure this stays that way."

A flicker of something akin to grudging respect flickered in Robbins's eyes, quickly replaced by a flicker of fear. "That's not all," he blurted out, the words tumbling over each other in a desperate rush. "There's more you need to know. I... I wasn't the only one involved. There's a whole network... Hydra, they call themselves... "

Brett's eyes narrowed sharply. "Hydra?" he echoed, the name sending a jolt through him. This was bigger than he ever imagined. "Tell me everything," he demanded, a new urgency rising in his voice. "Who else is involved? How deep does this rabbit hole go?"

The storm outside must have subsided, for an eerie kind of quiet had merged with the plush study. The senator, earlier a paradigm of power personified, was sitting hunched in his chair, a bundle of dispirited humanity with a beseeching look of anguish.

"The President," he croaked, the word escaping his lips like a confession whispered in the dead of night.

Brett's heart lurched. Disbelief and a morbid fascination warred within him. "The President?" he echoed, his voice barely a whisper. "You're saying the President... he's involved in this?"

Robbins nodded weakly, a tremor wracking his once-sturdy frame. "Yes. He's been playing both sides for years, feeding secrets to the highest bidder and lining his own pockets and those of his cronies. I was a fool to think I was above it all. Now, all I want is to see him brought down."

The weight of the revelation settled on Brett's shoulders like a leaden cloak. The highest office in the land is corrupted by greed and betrayal. The very foundation of national security is compromised by the man sworn to protect it. Fury, cold and raw, ignited within him. He yearned for justice, to purge this festering rot from the nation's heart.

"Tell me everything, you know," he demanded, his voice steely as he leaned forward, his gaze unwavering. "Every deal, every channel they used, the offshore accounts... everything."

Robbins swallowed hard, his throat rasping like sandpaper. "I was just a cog in their machine," he rasped, his voice laden with self-loathing. "But I can expose the whole operation—the shell companies they used to launder money, the coded messages they exchanged, the secret meetings they held behind closed doors. I can show you how they kept everything hidden and avoided detection for so long."

Brett's mind raced. This wasn't just about stolen secrets or a missing AI program anymore. It was about a systemic betrayal, a cancer that had burrowed deep into the heart of the government. But going public with such explosive accusations would be akin to setting off a political earthquake, potentially fracturing the nation and plunging it into chaos.

"What do you want, Senator?" he asked finally, his voice low and measured.

Robbins met his gaze, a flicker of desperation igniting in his bloodshot eyes. "Leniency," he pleaded. "A chance to redeem myself, to protect my family. I'm not a monster, Brett. I was blinded by ambition and seduced by the promise of power. But I can help make things right; be a witness and guide through this deceit labyrinth."

A tense silence descended upon the room, thick with the weight of Brett's decision. He understood the risks—the potential backlash, the storm of controversy that would engulf them all. But the alternative—allowing the president to continue his insidious game—was unthinkable.

"Alright, Senator," Brett conceded finally, his voice firm. "We'll talk. But understand this: your cooperation, your complete and unwavering cooperation, is only the beginning. You'll need to prove yourself, provide us with concrete evidence, and be prepared to face the consequences of your actions."

A flicker of relief washed over Robbins's face, a spark of hope battling the shame that clung to him like a shroud. "I'm ready," he rasped; his voice thick with newfound determination. "Tell me what I need to do. I'll tear this whole house of cards down, brick by agonizing brick."

The following conversation stretched well into the pre-dawn hours, a covert exchange of secrets and strategies whispered in hushed tones. Brett outlined a plan, a high-stakes operation requiring a team of his most trusted investigators, secure communication channels, and a carefully constructed network of informants. Robbins, fueled by a desperate need for redemption, spilled his knowledge, detailing the president's elaborate schemes, the hidden network of shell companies, and the coded messages that served as their currency of corruption.

As the first rays of dawn peeked through the windows, casting a pale golden light across the room, Brett knew this was just the beginning. The fight ahead would be fraught with danger, a high-wire act of shadows and secrets where every move could be their last. The stakes had never been higher. But armed with a confession and an unwavering sense of justice, Brett was ready to play this deadly game.

Chapter Fifteen:
Web Of Betrayal

Flashing red and blue lights painted the marbled lobby in an ominous glow. Henderson, the lead agent on the case, barked terse orders into his walkie-talkie, clearly supercharged with adrenaline. Across the hall, cameras were already swarming, their hungry lenses trained on the double oak doors leading to Senator Morrison's office.

"Alright, people, remember the plan," Henderson dismissed without even looking at his partner, Agent Smith, and the rest of the team. One deafening silence followed the other, interspersed only by the low hum of the air conditioning system. Then, with a battering ram in hand, they charged.

The door cracked from the doorframe with a loud bang. At the breaking of the door, Morrison was on his feet, the chair squealing across the floor. His face, which usually broke into cordial charm with practice, contorted into a look of disbelief. "What is the meaning of this?" he roared, his voice laced with a tremor that betrayed his bluster.

"Senator Morrison," Henderson said, his voice clipped and official, "you are under arrest for federal corruption charges."

Morrison's bluster evaporated, replaced by a cold, calculating look. "On what grounds?" he spat, his eyes darting around the room, searching for an escape.

"We have evidence, Senator," Agent Smith said, stepping forward, a file clutched in his hand. "Enough to put you away for a very long time."

The scene in Congressman Robbins' office played out with similar drama. But unlike Morrison's icy defiance, Robbins crumbled. His face paled, and he stuttered, his forehead drenched with sweat, his words becoming incoherent as he pleaded. "It wasn't me! I... I was set up!"

News of the arrests broke like a dam bursting. News channels exploded with live footage, reporters scrambling to piece together the story. The public, used to the carefully crafted personas these men had cultivated, reeled in shock.

Meanwhile, in a secure location, David Davis, the former Senator's aide turned star witness, huddled with the prosecution team. The weight of his decision pressed heavily on him. He had seen the monster underneath the Senator's refined façade, and he knew that his testimony was the ultimate way of exposing it.

"David, are you still sure about this?" the prosecutor stated, looking at him with a great deal of doubt.

David swallowed hard. "Yes," he replied. He spoke in a rather firm way despite his shaking hands. "The people deserve to know the truth."

The trial was a media mosh pit, feeding the connoisseurs of crisis their red meat. News vans lined the block. Satellite dishes sprouted from the roofs in a tangle of kudzu, turning every house in sight into a hostile nest of birds. Inside the courtroom, the atmosphere was thick and incredibly dense, and you could cut it into glass slices and serve it.

On one side sat Morrison and Robbins, their faces like thunderclouds. Gone were the practiced smiles and easy charm they'd used to navigate the halls of power. Now, they were cornered animals, their eyes darting nervously between the jury box and David Davis, who sat on the witness stand.

Davis, a slight man with haunted eyes, gripped the armrests, knuckles white. He'd spent weeks preparing for this moment, reliving the nightmare he'd endured working for Senator Morrison. Taking a deep breath, he began his testimony, his voice a steady counterpoint to the storm brewing in the room.

"The Senator..." Davis started, then paused, his gaze locking with Morrison's. The Senator's face contorted in a silent snarl, but Davis held his ground. "The Senator," he continued, his voice firm, "often made comments about needing additional funding for his re-election campaign. He'd hint at... favors... that could be done for him by certain... contributors."

The defense attorney, a silver-haired shark named Thomas, pounced. "Objection!" he boomed, his voice echoing in the tense courtroom. "Hearsay! My clients have a right to a fair trial, free from baseless accusations!"

The judge, a stern woman with a mane of iron-gray hair, pursed her lips. "Overruled, Mr. Thomas. Mr. Davis can elaborate on his experiences while employed by the Senator."

Thomas slammed his briefcase shut, a theatrical display of outrage. But the jury was watching Davis intently their faces etched with a mix of curiosity and dawning comprehension.

Over the next few days, Davis painted a damning picture of Morrison and Robbins's operation. He recounted late-night meetings filled with hushed tones and bulging envelopes, the casual disregard for the law that permeated their every action.

"One night," Davis said, his voice dropping to a low murmur, "I overheard the Senator talking to Congressman Robbins on the phone. They were discussing... a donation... from a company that had just been awarded a very lucrative government contract."

There was an audible gasp echoing in the court. The jury members leaned a little forward made everyone's eyes riveted to Davis. Even the judge was suddenly noticing everything unfolding in front of her.

Thomas sensed that the tide had turned against his people, and he now started to furiously cross-examine Davis. He badgered Davis, trying to poke holes in his story, discrediting him as a disgruntled ex-employee. But Davis held firm.

"I know, what I saw," he insisted, his voice gaining strength with every accusation. "I know, what I heard. And I will not be silenced."

The trial stretched on for weeks, each day a new revelation, a fresh piece of evidence chipping away at Morrison and Robbins's carefully constructed defenses. Finally, the day arrived for closing arguments.

The prosecutor, a young lady with rigidity and determination, addressed all the jurors.

"The evidence is clear," she declared, her voice ringing through the courtroom. "These men, entrusted with the public's trust, betrayed that trust for their own personal gain. They are not above the law. They are not untouchable."

In his closing argument, Thomas weaved a tale of political witch hunts and innocent men caught in a web of lies. But his words rang hollow compared to the weight of the evidence and the quiet dignity of David Davis.

The jury deliberated for what felt like an eternity. Then, finally, the verdict came in. "Guilty," the foreman announced, his voice heavy with finality.

As the words hung in the air, a wave of relief washed over the courtroom. Justice, though delayed, had prevailed.

Morrison and Robbins were limp in their chairs, their faces pale. Once powerful men were now poor convicts with a record. Their character, which they had created for their public image, politely faded away like a mirage in the desert.

The moment they were taken into the police van with handcuffs, a flash of cameras appeared, documenting their disgrace for eternity. The image – two fallen idols, their arrogance stripped bare – served as a stark reminder of the power of truth and the importance of holding even the most powerful accountable.

In the aftermath of the trial, David Davis became an unlikely hero. His story, one of courage and whistleblowing, resonated with the public. He received countless letters of gratitude from people who thanked him for standing up for what was right.

Though forever marked by his experience, Davis found solace in the knowledge that he had made a difference. He had helped expose corruption and ensure that justice was served. And in that, he found a measure of peace.

***

The President of the United States (POTUS) held barely the totality of power and importance, and his career as a politician lasted for around 40 years. He had a faithful audience, and his charisma and charm hypnotized them. However, underneath his charismatic exterior, there was a dirty and terrible secret hidden.

Unbeknownst to the people, POTUS's life of corruption did not stay within the boundaries of his own country; rather, it spread across the borders as well. For a long time, he has been conducting a highly sophisticated deal involving governments of foreigners offering bribes for the extension of favorable conditions and policies. He built the web of scandal very skillfully, hiding the shell companies, offshore bank accounts, and loyal associates.

At the center of the undercover business was Marcus Stein, a sharp-witted entrepreneur and one of the president's trusted comrades. Their conversations were all in hushed tones and cunning plans as they plotted ways to clean up the dirty cash and camouflage the money trail.

Meanwhile, Li Yang, a cunning and ambitious diplomat from a foreign power, acted as the President's secret ally. Their conversations were shrouded in secrecy, discussing trade deals and financial advantages, all in exchange for the steady flow of bribes. They were intoxicated by their power, seeing themselves as undefeated.

As time went by, the appetite for power and accumulation of wealth in the President turned out to be insatiable. His conversations with his co-conspirators were filled with greed and ambition; their plans reaching far beyond the borders of their own country. They reveled in their secrecy, believing that they were invincible.

The late-night hum of the White House was a constant thrumming in President's ears. His shoulders hunch as he leans forward towards the Resolute Desk with a worry line etched on his forehead. Not even the Tiffany lamp, the soft glow of which could not strain the shadows that seemed to draft him as if a funereal cloth would do.

A piercing squeak cut through the stillness. It wasn't his usual phone; this was a secure line, one reserved for a select few. Nate snatched it up, his voice a low rasp.

"Mr. President," a smooth, accented voice purred from the other end. It was Wei, the Chinese official Nate had been cultivating for months. "The transfer is complete. The path is open."

Nate gripped the phone so hard his knuckles turned white. "Excellent work, Wei. They'll never suspect a thing." A tight smile stretched across his face, hidden by the shadows. The weight in his gut, however, refused to ease. This deal, this web of deceit he'd woven, felt more like a tightening noose around his neck with every passing moment.

Months bled into weeks, the air thick with anticipation. Then, the green light. A coded message from Wei arrived: "Operation Osprey is a go."

Nate retreated to his private study, a hidden war room within the White House. On a secure line, he dialed a number memorized with excruciating detail.

"The Banker," the voice on the other end answered, a husky rasp devoid of warmth. This was no ordinary financier; this was Nate's shadow operator, a man who dealt in the murkiest corners of the financial world.

"Time to move, my friend," Nate said, his voice clipped. "Osprey takes flight at dawn. Transfer the funds discreetly. Multiple offshore accounts, shell companies – the usual dance. Leave no trace, no breadcrumbs back to the States."

A low chuckle emanated from the phone. "You know I excel at the disappearing act, Mr. President. Consider it done." The Banker's voice held a dangerous edge, a hint of something more than simple business. Nate felt a prickle of unease but quickly pushed it down. He couldn't afford second thoughts now.

He could feel the hammer strike his nerves, each second a blow in his already ruined, trembling mind. He was a man gambling with a high risk, and losing was unbearable. It was a struggle for survival for the presidency, and for the country's future; it was a matter of life and death. As dawn painted the sky a pale orange, Nate knew the line between power and destruction had been irrevocably crossed. This game of shadows was getting intense.

Chapter Sixteen:
Secrecy And Celebration

In a secluded back room of a high-end steakhouse, the air hung heavy with the scent of aged leather and thinly veiled paranoia. President, eyes flitting around the room like a cornered animal, addressed his conspirators – a motley crew bound by greed and ambition.

"Gentlemen," President began, his voice low and raspy, "our little dance with the Chinese has been a lucrative one. But let's not get cocky." He shot a pointed look at his nephew, Paul, a young man with a face already etched with the cynicism of a seasoned politician.

"We all know the score," Paul drawled, leaning back in his chair. "This gravy train can't keep chugging if your term ends." His gaze flickered to a large world map sprawled across the table, dotted with colored pins marking their hidden accounts and investments.

"Precisely," President hissed, his hand hovering over a red pin marking a particularly juicy account in the Cayman Islands. "That's why we need a fail-safe. A way to keep the money flowing, discreetly, long after I'm out of office."

A man named Stein, a financial guru with a reputation as shady as his pinstripe suit, chuckled from behind a thick cigar. "Leave it to us, Mr. President. We've set up a network of intermediaries – ghosts, really – who'll cancel the cash trail before it can lead back to any of us."

"Cryptocurrency," chimed in the Secretary of State, a woman whose morals seemed as flexible as her allegiance. "We've linked digital wallets to various platforms, perfect for receiving anonymous payments."

A sense of smug satisfaction filled the room, a poisonous miasma that reeked of their shared ambition. "This web we've woven," the Secretary of State continued, a triumphant glint in her eyes, "is as intricate as it is untraceable. Our identities and ill-gotten gains will remain comfortably hidden."

Weeks later, in a sterile vault of an offshore bank, a nameless account pulsed to life. A faceless treasurer spoke in a clipped monotone to his unseen colleagues, "Funds are in transit, gentlemen. The President's nest egg is secure."

Back in the States, a different kind of meeting was underway. In the hushed privacy of a hidden residence, President huddled with his most trusted lieutenant, a high-ranking White House Czar who held the key to another one of the President's secrets: stolen classified files, bartered for with the Chinese in exchange for lucrative contracts.

The air crackled with nervous energy, the stench of greed, and deceit thick enough to choke on. They all knew that the precariousness of their situation. One wrong move, one leak, and their carefully constructed house of cards would come tumbling down.

President, his voice a low growl, addressed the group. "We've played the good puppets for the Chinese long enough, securing them contracts and undermining national security for their fat paychecks. But have they held up their end of the bargain?"

Paul, ever the pragmatist, chimed in, "Relax, Uncle. We've made our expectations crystal clear. The gravy train keeps moving, even after you're out." He raised a glass of the finest vintage, a sardonic smile playing on his lips.

"To a profitable partnership," President echoed, clinking glasses with his co-conspirators. One by one, they followed suit, each toast a chilling reminder of their twisted pact, a pact built on betrayal and fueled by an insatiable hunger for wealth and power.

***

Months later, in the sterile vault of a Swiss bank, a symphony of clicks and whirring fans filled the air as the treasurer executed the withdrawal. With a final tap on the keyboard, he announced to his unseen associates, "The funds are ready for delivery, gentlemen. A veritable king's ransom – cash, gold, silver, the very blood of our operation, and of course, the untraceable ghost in the machine – cryptocurrency."

News of the transfer reached President within hours. He convened another clandestine meeting with his co-conspirators, a gathering shrouded in shadows and paranoia. Raising a glass of aged whiskey,

President initiated the toast, his voice dripping with a chilling satisfaction, "To the hidden wealth that fuels our power, the invisible hand that shapes the world to our desires."

His cohorts echoed the toast with grim fervor. The President's U.S. partner, a man whose loyalty was as questionable as his morals, followed suit. "To the twisted web of deception we've woven," he declared, his voice raspy with a hint of unease. "May it forever conceal the secrets that bind us."

Paul, ever the pragmatist, offered his own toast, a cynical smile playing on his lips. "To the enduring success of our partnership," he proclaimed, "a testament to our shared ambition and unwavering greed."

Months bled into weeks; each day a nerve-wracking exercise in patience. In a private residence far removed from the prying eyes of Washington, a team of specialists meticulously transformed the raw funds – a grotesque alchemy that saw mountains of cash morph into inconspicuous luxury items. Sparkling diamonds became silent testaments to their crimes, while priceless works of art served as elaborate money laundering vessels.

"Everything secure?" Paul inquired, his voice laced with a tremor of anxiety.

The man overseeing the operation, a notorious smuggler with ice-cold blue eyes, offered a curt nod. "Disguised flawlessly, Mr. President. No trace of their illicit origins will remain."

With the funds now disguised as legitimate assets, the President's U.S. partner flew to a secluded offshore location to oversee the final act. Here, in a hidden fortress of finance, the ill-gotten gains were layered with shell companies, anonymous trusts, and a labyrinthine network of financial transactions. Each step is meticulously documented; each transfer a further obfuscation of the trail leading back to them.

"The final layer of protection," he muttered to himself, a hint of triumph creeping into his voice.

Back in Washington, President sat alone in the Oval Office, the weight of his betrayal pressing down on him like a physical burden. He gazed out the window at the bustling city below, a city he now saw as a playground for his avarice. A self-satisfied smirk played on his lips.

"Blissfully unaware," he murmured, his voice tinged with a dangerous edge. "The American people remain oblivious to the empire we've built on lies."

His trusted confidante, the White House Czar, materialized from the shadows. "Mr. President," he said, his voice a low rasp, "our deception plan remains unbreakable. We've secured our future and theirs."

Meanwhile, a world away, another kind of operation was underway. In a dimly lit backroom far removed from the halls of power, a man known only as "Banker 1" orchestrated the final phase of the money laundering. With each transaction and each transfer of ill-gotten wealth, he pushed the funds further and further out of reach of the authorities. Finally, with a satisfied grunt, he completed the transfer.

"The money's heading stateside," he rasped into a secure phone; his voice devoid of emotion. "They'll never see it coming."

Across the continent, in a plush D.C., law office, a trusted attorney orchestrated the final flourish. With a flourish, he signed a document, sealing the iron-clad agreement that secured their ill-gotten gains behind the veil of attorney-client privilege.

"Our power remains protected," he declared, a chilling smile playing on his lips.

***

A grim smile stretched across Minister Wu's face as the secure video call connected him with his counterparts in Beijing. "Operation Osprey has landed," he announced, his voice laced with a predator's satisfaction. "The Americans remain blissfully ignorant, blinded by their insatiable hunger for immediate gratification."

A chorus of murmurs rippled through the screen. General Li, a man whose weathered face held the weight of decades spent strategizing, leaned forward. "The short-sightedness of the West is both their weakness and our greatest advantage," he rumbled. "They chase fleeting trends while we play the long game, a game measured in centuries."

"Indeed," Minister Wu agreed, a glint in his eyes. "Their 'Belt and Road' initiative? A Trojan horse, willingly funded by their own greed. Soon, the American economy will be so deeply intertwined with ours that they'll be dancing to our tune."

A younger official, his ambition barely concealed, piped up. "And what of the loose ends? The President's...associates?"

Minister Wu's smile vanished, replaced by a steely glint. "The attorney has secured the final distribution. Attorney-client privilege, a beautiful veil that will keep our involvement hidden."

Across the ocean, in the dimly lit confines of the Oval Office, President swirled the amber liquid in his glass, a storm brewing behind his eyes. The weight of the buried secret, the ever-present fear of exposure, gnawed at him. He glanced at the Czar, a silent question hanging in the air.

"Our tracks are covered," the Czar rasped, his voice devoid of warmth. "For now."

President wasn't convinced. A prickle of unease ran down his spine. Somewhere, a single misstep, a single misplaced thread in their web of deceit, could unravel it all.

***

Four months had crawled by, each day a tense balancing act on a knife's edge. The President, paranoia gnawing at his insides, summoned his inner circle to a secluded hunting lodge nestled deep within the Montana wilderness. Gone were the opulent backrooms and private residences; here, amidst the rugged terrain and watchful eyes of mounted trophies, a sense of desperate urgency hung heavy in the air.

"Gentlemen," the President rasped, his voice barely a whisper above the crackling fireplace, "we have a problem. Tehran... they're getting restless. The promised funds haven't materialized, and whispers of dissent are starting to reach my ears."

A collective grimace rippled across the room. Paul, his youthful features etched with a cynical mask, was the first to speak. "Mr. President, throwing them a bone is one thing, but a significant amount? We need a damn good story, one that wouldn't raise eyebrows even with a magnifying glass."

"The Ukrainian model," chimed in Stein, the financial guru; his voice a gravelly rasp. "It worked flawlessly for years. Funnel the money through humanitarian aid, a gesture of goodwill disguised as a national security move."

A predatory glint flickered in the President's eyes. "Excellent, Stein. We'll play the humanitarian card. Announce an executive order – Iran's nuclear program a potential threat, blah, blah, blah. Disguised aid to encourage disarmament."

A chorus of murmurs of approval echoed through the room. The State Department's representative, a man whose loyalty was as easily swayed as a weather vane, nodded vigorously. "We can draft a convincing press release, highlight the urgency of the situation."

"And the Justice Department?" the President inquired, his gaze flickering to the other corrupt official in the room.

The official, a once-respected figure now twisted by greed, cleared his throat. "My department will ensure the transfer goes through all legal channels, of course. No red flags, no unnecessary scrutiny."

"We need more than just the existing channels," a U.S. partner, a weathered man whose morals had long been eroded by ambition, pointed out. "Let's set up a smokescreen – a fake charity organization. Funneling some of the payoffs through a seemingly noble cause would be the perfect camouflage."

Heads bobbed in agreement. The corrupt lawyers, their ethics as flexible as a rubber band, eagerly embraced the challenge. Soon, a meticulously crafted facade – a charity dedicated to global peace and understanding – took shape. Accountants cooked the books, lawyers drafted impressive mission statements, and a website boasting heartwarming testimonials materialized out of thin air.

***

A triumphant grin stretched across the President's face as a holographic map of the world flickered to life in the secure meeting room. Lines traced the flow of billions from their hidden accounts to Tehran, a crimson tide symbolizing their illicit gains.

"Gentlemen," he purred, his voice dripping with a predator's satisfaction, "we've pulled it off. Billions funneled right under the noses of the American people, all disguised as a noble act of diplomacy."

Paul, the President's ever-loyal nephew, leaned back in his chair, a sly smile playing on his lips. "Our network of shell companies worked like a charm," he declared. "Corporations within corporations, layers upon layers of obfuscation. The kickbacks are flowing like a well-oiled machine."

The U.S. partner; a man with eyes as cold as the steel he once traded, nodded curtly. "The intermediaries have done their part," he confirmed. "Our identities are as secure as a vault buried a mile deep."

A sense of exhilaration rippled through the room. The President, emboldened by their success, slammed his fist on the table. "Remember," he boomed; his voice echoing in the sterile room, "five to ten percent of that money will find its way back to us. Cash, gold, the finest art the world has to offer – nothing will be off-limits. No trace, no suspicion, just pure, unadulterated wealth."

Suddenly, a sharp buzz pierced the celebratory atmosphere. A corrupt banker, his face illuminated by the soft glow of his encrypted phone, glanced at the message displayed on the screen. "The funds are ready for distribution," he announced, his voice devoid of emotion.

Across the globe, in a plush office overlooking the bustling streets of Tehran, an Iranian official cradled the phone to his ear, a satisfied smirk playing on his lips. "The money has arrived," he purred, his voice smooth as oil. "You Americans have been remarkably discreet."

"We've done our part," came the clipped reply from the American intermediary on the other end. "Just make sure the kickbacks start rolling in soon, and keep them discreet."

Days bled into weeks, and the President's Oval Office became a haven for whispered celebrations. "The money's flowing like a river, gentlemen," the President declared with a wide smile revealing a predator's glint in his eyes. "The kickbacks are here, just as promised. Greed, power, control – that's what this game is all about, isn't it?"

"Flawless," Paul chimed in, his youthful face flushed with a mixture of excitement and avarice. "No loose ends, no suspicion. Mr. President, I can leverage your newfound influence for years to come, selling access to the highest bidder."

The Secretary of State, a woman whose loyalty was as easily swayed as a weather vane in a hurricane, leaned forward, her voice oozing with false confidence. "Our layers of secrecy are impregnable, Mr. President. We are untouchable."

Meanwhile, in the sterile confines of a Swiss bank, a scene unfolded that would shatter their illusion of invincibility. A symphony of clicks and whirring fans filled the air as the treasurer executed a colossal withdrawal – a king's ransom in cash, gold, silver, and the ever-elusive cryptocurrency.

"The funds are ready for delivery," he announced, his voice flat, devoid of any moral qualms. Little did he know, unseen eyes were watching, meticulously documenting every detail of the transaction.

On the other side of the world, in a hidden offshore safe-house, a team of specialists worked diligently, meticulously transforming the raw funds into a facade of opulence. Cash morphed into sparkling diamonds, while priceless works of art became elaborate vessels for money laundering. Each step, each transformation, was another layer of deception, another brick in the ever-growing wall of their criminal enterprise.

Back in Washington D.C., beneath the very seat of power itself, a hidden meeting room buzzed with activity. The President and his inner circle, oblivious to the storm brewing on the horizon, received a detailed report on the incoming kickbacks.

"The operation is running smoothly," the President declared, a self-satisfied smirk playing on his lips. "The American people remain blissfully ignorant, fattened on lies and empty promises."

"Cash, gold, crypto - it's a never-ending stream of wealth," Paul crowed, his voice thick with unrestrained greed. "We're becoming richer by the hour."

The U.S., partner, ever the pragmatist, raised a glass in a chilling toast. "Our web of deceit is intricate, a masterpiece of manipulation. No one will ever be able to unravel it."

As the President and his band of thieves raised their crystal flutes in a toast to their untouchable empire, a flurry of activity unfolded far beyond the opulent confines of the meeting room. In the labyrinthine underbelly of the global financial system, a network of shadowy figures sprang into action.

In a dingy backroom of a Hong Kong karaoke bar, a triad boss barked orders into a burner phone. His call connected to a discreet money exchange in Dubai, where weathered bills were meticulously swapped for crisp, unmarked Euros. The illicit funds then embarked on a digital odyssey, bouncing through a labyrinth of anonymous cryptocurrency wallets, each transaction adding another layer of obfuscation.

Across the Atlantic, a team of hackers in a nondescript Eastern European building intercepted a seemingly innocuous email attachment. Within its code, they unearthed a hidden message – a digital breadcrumb leading them to a network of offshore bank accounts teeming with suspicious activity.

Meanwhile, in a bustling shipping yard on the coast of Singapore, a nondescript container was loaded onto a freighter bound for Miami. Its manifest listed innocuous office supplies, but a keen eye would have noticed the tell-tale signs of a meticulously crafted false flag – a desperate attempt to disguise a shipment of priceless, ill-gotten art.

The clock was ticking. Each step that the President's ill-gotten gains, took further down the laundering pipeline added another layer of complexity, another hurdle for those determined to expose the truth.

Chapter Seventeen: Impeachment

Rain hammered against the bulletproof glass of the interrogation room. Inside, the fluorescent lights cast a harsh glare on the two gaunt figures across the table from Doctor Brett. Senator Robbins, normally impeccably dressed, looked haggard in a rumpled prison jumpsuit. His face was lined with worry, and Congressman Morrison kept fidgeting with his handcuffs.

"Let's cut to the chase, gents," Brett said, leaning forward. What game are you playing here? Are you offering to sing on the President for a lighter sentence? You two were the Teflon Kings, untouchable. Now this?"

A bitter laugh escaped Robbins. "Teflon wears thin, Doctor. Especially in prison showers." He took a deep breath. "Look, we're not spinning yarns. The President's been neck-deep in the same pond we were swimming in."

Brett raised an eyebrow. "Selling secrets, influence, the whole nine yards? Sounds far-fetched. You know the implications of an accusation like that."

Morrison slammed his palm on the table, the metal clanging. "Implication? Hell, Doctor, we've got proof. Bank statements, coded messages, the whole damn network. We were puppets, Brett, dancing to his tune while he kept the strings."

Intrigued, Brett leaned back. "Alright, let's hear it. Proof you can back up these claims. And no more riddles."

Robbins sighed, his eyes hardening. "Remember the Panama Project leak? All that dirty money hidden in offshore accounts? That wasn't just some random billionaire's playground. It was POTUS's personal treasure trove."

The President's initials hung heavy in the air. Brett felt a thrill course through him. This could be bigger than anything he'd ever dealt with.

"How do you know?"

"Because, we were the ones setting it up for him," Morrison said, his voice low. "Shell companies, dummy accounts, you name it. We were the ones laundering the funds from those 'classified briefings' he kept holding with foreign dignitaries."

An image flashed in Brett's mind – a late-night news clip of the President meeting behind closed doors with a group of shadowy figures. "And how do you know those briefings weren't legitimate?"

"Because they weren't!" Robbins spat. "We saw the transcripts. They were coded messages, bartering top-secret intel for hefty payoffs in those offshore accounts."

A cold dread settled in Brett's stomach. If true; this was a political earthquake waiting to happen.

"This... this is mind blowing," Brett said, his voice barely a whisper. "You understand what you're doing? Turning your back on your own party, going after the most powerful man in the country?"

"Powerful, maybe," Robbins said, a ghost of a smile playing on his lips. "But not invincible. We're done taking the fall for his schemes. About time he answers for his own sins."

"Fine," Brett said, determination hardening his voice. Give me everything you have—every conversation, every message, every trace. This goes beyond you two. This is about national security."

Over the next few hours, a story of greed and corruption unfolded. Codes were deciphered, bank statements analyzed, and a meticulously crafted web of deceit was laid bare. By the time dawn broke, Brett had enough to launch a full-blown investigation.

But pulling down the President wasn't going to be easy. Leaks were inevitable. Whispers reached the White House first. A phone call crackled in Brett's ear, the President's voice dripping with venom.

"Doctor, I hear that you've been busy digging into some very thin air. Let me suggest you find a new hobby before you drown in quicksand."

Brett slammed the phone down, his jaw clenched. He knew the threat was real. There would be pressure, attempts to bury the investigation, and maybe even threats to his own life. But looking at the faces of Robbins and Morrison, two men broken by a system, they helped create, he knew, he couldn't back down.

This wasn't just about revenge for them. It was about holding the highest office accountable. In the coming storm, Brett knew he needed every ally he could muster. He picked up a black phone and dialed a number. "Agent Smith? We need to talk."

The air in the dimly lit conference room hung heavy. Agent Smith, his steely gaze fixed on the faces gathered around the table, spoke in a low voice. "Gentlemen, the walls are closing in. Leaks. The President knows, we're onto him."

A tense silence followed. Agent Henderson slammed his fist on the table. "Dammit! We need to move fast. Every day we wait, the deeper he digs himself in."

"Agreed," said Lt. General Adams, his weathered face grim. "But rushing in with half-baked evidence is suicide. The public opinion polls are already shifting. They're buying his spin."

The President had indeed gone on the offensive. A carefully orchestrated media blitz portrayed him as the victim of a partisan witch hunt. His loyal attack dogs in Congress were in full cry, spewing accusations and casting doubt on the task force's motives.

"We need something big," Smith said, tapping a file on the table. "Something undeniable."

The room erupted in a flurry of ideas. Hours melted away as they dissected evidence, debated strategies, and strategized counter-moves. Finally, Henderson leaned back in his chair, a flicker of determination in his eyes. "There's a lead. A banker in Zurich. He's been flagged for suspicious activity – large, irregular deposits into accounts linked to shell companies."

"Shell companies?" Smith raised an eyebrow. "That could be promising. Let's see what we can dig up."

The next day, Smith and Henderson found themselves in a sterile office overlooking the bustling streets of Zurich. They sat across from a nervous-looking man, Herr Schmidt; a mid-level banker at a prestigious Swiss bank.

"Mr. Schmidt," Henderson began, leaning forward, "we appreciate you taking the time to meet with us."

Schmidt cleared his throat, his gaze darting between the two Americans. "Of course. Anything to help with... uh... your inquiries."

Smith placed a photo on the table. A picture of the President, his face etched with a smile, shaking hands with a well-dressed Asian businessman. "Recognize this gentleman?"

Schmidt's face drained of color. "That's... that's Mr. Li. From China Prosperity Holdings."

"And these accounts?" Henderson slid a file across the table. "Do any of them ring a bell?"

Schmidt's hands trembled as he scanned the document. A single bead of sweat trickled down his temple. "I... I can't say for sure. Banking privacy laws..."

"Let's cut to the chase, Mr. Schmidt," Smith said, his voice turning steely. "These accounts are linked to a series of highly suspicious transactions. Millions of dollars funneled from offshore havens, all landing in the same place – accounts connected to the President."

Silence hung heavy in the air. Schmidt licked his dry lips. "I... I may be able to provide some... additional information. Unofficially, of course."

Henderson exchanged a glance with Smith. This was it. Their moment of truth.

Under the cloak of night, in a safe house mile away from Zurich, Schmidt spilled his guts. He revealed a network of shell companies meticulously crafted to funnel illicit funds from foreign governments into the President's personal coffers. He spoke of coded messages, clandestine meetings, and a web of corruption that ran deeper than anyone could have imagined.

With this bombshell testimony, the task force had their smoking gun. They presented their findings to the Speaker of the House, a man with a steely glint in his eyes and a deep respect for the law.

"This is treason," the Speaker declared, his voice thunderous. "The President has committed a grave betrayal. We must act swiftly, decisively."

The wheels of justice began to turn. The House Judiciary Committee convened, and Senator Robbins, gaunt and pale, stood before them. His voice, though shaky, carried the weight of truth as he detailed the President's treachery.

The nation watched, transfixed. The President's carefully constructed facade began to crumble. His attacks on Robbins as a vengeful traitor now rang hollow. The tide of public opinion started to shift.

The storm had arrived. The President's world was imploding, and the task force, battered but unbowed, watched as the walls finally closed in on him.

Chapter Eighteen:
Political Ripples

The pre-dawn sky bled a pale orange as Dr. Brett Evans surveyed the scene. Operation Blind Allegiance, the culmination of a year-long investigation, was about to go live. "Alright team," he addressed his task force, a mix of crack investigators and financial forensics experts. "Senator Robbins' estate is heavily fortified. Expect resistance. We need to secure the premises and get to his financial records before they disappear."

A grim determination settled over the team. The evidence they'd gathered pointed toward a web of corruption that ran deep, reaching all the way to the Oval Office. Senator Robbins, once a golden boy of politics, had become a key witness, his testimony a potential bombshell.

Across town, Special Agent Ramirez barked orders, his voice a steady counterpoint to the thrumming tension. The President's residence was a fortress swarming with Secret Service agents. Their mission was riskier, a direct assault on the highest office in the land.

The clock ticked down, each second stretching into an eternity. Finally, the signal crackled through their comms – "Showtime."

Evans took a deep breath, adrenaline coursing through him. With a battering ram leading the charge, his team breached the Senator's estate gates. Alarms blared, shattering the pre-dawn quiet. Two burly security guards emerged; guns drawn. A brief, chaotic firefight erupted, before they were subdued.

Inside the opulent mansion, the air hung thick with the scent of panic. Dr. Evans and his team fanned out. Upstairs, in the master bedroom, they found the Senator, a pale ghost of his former self, huddled in a corner.

"Senator Robbins," Evans said cautiously, approaching him with his hands raised. "We're here to help."

Robbins looked up, his eyes hollow. "Help? After I spilled my guts?"

"There's no turning back now, Senator," Evans said, his voice firm but reassuring. "We need your help to get this evidence out."

As his team secured the rest of the house, Evans and another investigator, a steely-eyed woman named Emily, began questioning Robbins. Details tumbled out – secret meetings, coded messages, and a meticulously crafted network of offshore accounts. Each revelation chipped away at the carefully constructed facade of the President's administration.

Meanwhile, across the city, chaos unfolded at the White House. Special Agent Mark Ramirez and his team overwhelmed the Secret Service using flashbangs and practiced maneuvers. Inside, they found the President, his face contorted in rage, surrounded by his advisors.

"Mr. President," Ramirez announced, his voice laced with steel, "you're under arrest for conspiracy, treason, and financial crimes."

The President roared, a caged animal. "This is a witch hunt! A political coup! You won't get away with this!"

Ignoring the President's tirade, Ramirez and his men secured the premises, confiscating electronic devices and searching for incriminating documents. The evidence they found mirrored what Evans' team was uncovering – a tangled web of corruption that stretched from the Oval Office to the highest echelons of international finance.

As dawn broke, the news of the raids exploded. Televisions blared, newspapers scrambled for updates, and social media erupted in a frenzy. The once-unthinkable - an operation targeting both the President and a key witness - had become a reality.

Back at the Senator's estate, Evans finished securing the critical evidence. He looked at Robbins, a flicker of respect in his eyes. "You did the right thing coming forward, Senator."

Robbins offered a wan smile. "I had no choice. This country deserves better than a conman in the Oval Office."

With the evidence secured and dawn breaking, a new chapter began. The battle lines were drawn, the fate of the presidency hanging in the balance. The road to justice would be long and arduous, filled with political machinations and legal battles. But with the damning evidence in hand, Dr. Evans and his team had ignited a firestorm that threatened to consume the highest office in the land. Their coordinated strike was just the first blow in a fight against a web of corruption that ran deeper than anyone could have imagined.

"Fan out!" Evans barked, the mansion echoing with the thud of boots on polished marble. His team, a well-oiled machine at this point, moved with practiced precision. Each room became a potential crime scene, every creaking floorboard a possible booby trap.

The air hung heavy with the stale scent of wealth – a strange combination of expensive cologne, and furniture polish. It felt suffocating, contrasting starkly with the adrenaline coursing through Evans' veins. This was it. The culmination of months of relentless pursuit.

A hidden compartment behind a tapestry revealed a room crammed with cash. Crisp bills, stacked floor to ceiling in perfect rows, and emanated an unsettling green glow in the harsh flashlight beams. The team escaped with a collective gasp as the enormity of the hidden wealth sunk in.

"This isn't just political corruption," Emily muttered, her voice tight with disbelief. "This is... this is pathological."

Evans ran a gloved hand down the stacks, a shiver running down his spine. This was not just greed; it was a grotesque obsession. It was a mirrored image of the scene they had received intel on: a hidden vault, also similarly overflowing with gold bars, found in a warehouse linked to the President.

They made their way into every room, in which there appeared to be a Pandora's box of potential. The master bedroom was truly the master. Clothes and shoes had been on display like those high-end department stores. Then, there was this well-hidden compartment that could only be noted after careful scrutiny. Inlaid within velvet drawers sat diamonds that sparkled with an obscene brilliance.

"These stones have to be worth millions," Emily said, her voice a hushed whisper.

Evans merely nodded, his stomach roiling. These were not just ill-gotten gains; they were glittering evidence of a web of corruption that stretched far beyond any one man.

He had the fleet of luxury cars, from the sleek Bentleys to the stately vintage Rolls Royce's, lit up in the unforgiving overhead lights of the cavernous garage—a monument to the Senator's insatiable appetite for expensive toys. Unlike other parts of the house, which bore evidence of meticulous care, there was a light layer of dust on some of them—that telltale hint of desperation in their acquisition.

"Looks like, he was running out of time to flaunt his loot," observed Emily.

Evans couldn't shake off the feeling that this was only the tip of the iceberg as his house was secured. Such luxury and such desperate attempts to hide it all spoke of a fear much greater than any legal consequences.

Meanwhile, across town, the FBI's raid on the White House mirrored the discoveries at the Senator's estate. Behind meticulously crafted portraits of past presidents lay hidden compartments overflowing with cash and gold. A team of tech specialists swarmed the President's private study, their fingers flying across keyboards as they cracked encrypted servers.

"Bingo!" John Carter, announced with a triumphant grin. "Found a treasure trove of crypto wallets. Looks like he's been playing the digital currency market too."

Sarah Miller, leaned closer. "Traceable?"

Carter shook his head. "Not easily. These wallets are masked with layers of anonymity software. But we can track the transactions."

Carter nodded, a grim satisfaction settling on his face. This wasn't just about stolen money; it was about the potential for foreign influence, a digital trail leading to a shadowy network of international players.

News of the raids spread like wildfire. The nation watched, transfixed, as the once-untouchable halls of power crumbled under the weight of evidence. The carefully constructed facade of the President and the Senator had been shattered, revealing a staggering house of secrets. The fight for justice had only just begun, and the evidence they'd uncovered was the first weapon in a war against a corruption that ran far deeper than anyone could have imagined. The walls were closing in, and the secrets they held threatened to bring the entire system down.

The White House press room crackled with a nervous energy that could be bottled. Cameras flashed like lightning as Ella Maxfield, the President's beleaguered press secretary, took the podium. Her usually perfectly coiffed hair seemed to wilt under the weight of scrutiny.

Gone was the practiced smile, replaced by a mask of forced composure that couldn't hide the tremor in her voice. This wasn't a routine press conference. This was a desperate attempt at damage control in the face of a political earthquake.

"Good afternoon," Maxfield began, her voice barely a whisper. The room erupted in a cacophony of shouts.

"Ms. Maxfield! Can you comment on the raids at the President's residence and Senator Robbins' estate?" a veteran reporter bellowed.

Ella, her eyes flitting nervously across the room, ignored the question. "The President has requested that I address the... recent developments," she stammered.

"Recent developments? You mean the mountain of evidence suggesting your boss is a common crook?" barked a reporter known for his biting wit.

Ella Maxfield flinched but continued, reading from a well-worn script. "'The President categorically denies any wrongdoing. These allegations are politically motivated and entirely without merit. The President has always conducted his financial affairs in an ethical and lawful manner.'"

A collective groan rose from the assembled press corps. This was the same canned response they'd heard for weeks, a blatant lie exposed by the mountains of incriminating evidence – secret bank accounts overflowing with cash, coded messages exchanged with foreign dignitaries, and a trail of dirty money leading straight back to the Oval Office.

"Are you seriously asking us to believe that a hidden vault filled with millions in cash and a room stacked floor-to-ceiling with gold bars is the epitome of 'ethical financial affairs'?" a female reporter pressed, her voice dripping with sarcasm.

Ella's carefully constructed facade crumbled. A bead of sweat trickled down her temple. "I... I can't comment on alleged details of the investigation," she stammered.

"But you can comment on the President's defiance?" another reporter interjected, his voice laced with anger. "Does the President have any intention of resigning in the face of this overwhelming evidence?"

The room held its breath. Maxfield's silence spoke volumes. Sweat soaked through her blouse, a stark contrast to the pristine White House podium. This wasn't a press conference anymore; it was an execution.

The President's carefully crafted web of lies was unraveling with each passing second. The evidence was irrefutable – a paper trail leading to offshore accounts, recordings of hushed phone calls with foreign leaders, and financial transactions that defied any shred of legitimacy.

Back in his office, the President watched the press conference with a growing sense of desperation. The man who had once exuded an aura of invincibility now resembled a cornered animal, his face pale and drawn.

"They're going to crucify me," he muttered, his voice laced with a newfound vulnerability.

His advisors exchanged worried glances. The jig was up. The media frenzy was just the beginning.

Chapter Nineteen:
President's Desperation

A collective gasp rippled through the press room as a seasoned reporter, Martha Kent, leaned into her microphone. "Ms. Wayne," she said, her voice laced with steel, "surely you can understand why the public is concerned about these allegations? The Treasury Department itself has flagged over 170 suspicious activity reports tied to the President. That's not something you can spin away with a press release."

Sweat beaded on Ella Wayne's forehead despite the arctic chill of the room. "We are cooperating fully with the investigation," she stammered, her voice cracking. "The President has nothing to hide. He is confident he will be cleared of any wrongdoing."

Ella's words lacked their usual conviction, ringing hollow in the tense atmosphere. A murmur of disbelief swept through the room.

"But if, and that's a very big if," Martha pressed, her gaze unwavering, "if the investigation confirms the findings of the House Committee, will the President resign?"

Ella's composure finally shattered. A flicker of panic crossed her eyes before she slammed her hand down on the podium. "We are not going to speculate on hypotheticals!" she snapped. "The President is focused on serving the American people, and carrying out his duties as President."

The room erupted in a cacophony of shouts. The carefully crafted narrative of a witch hunt was crumbling before their very eyes.

Across town, in the Oval Office, the President watched the press conference unfold, his face a mask of pale fury. The polished veneer of confidence he'd cultivated was peeling away, revealing a man on the verge of collapse. He slammed his fist on the Resolute Desk, the sound echoing through the cavernous room.

"This is a nightmare," he muttered; the words laced with a tremor of fear he hadn't felt since he was a child.

His advisors, a once-confident group of political sharks, now resembled cornered rats. The meticulously constructed web of lies they'd woven was unraveling at an alarming rate. 170 suspicious activity reports – that was a bombshell they couldn't defuse.

"Mr. President," Senator Evelyn finally dared to speak, her voice tight with worry. "The public mood has shifted. Your approval ratings are plummeting. We're losing allies by the hour."

The President let out a humorless bark of a laugh. "Allies? They were never allies, Evelyn. Just opportunists clinging to power." He ran a hand through his already disheveled hair. "What have I done?"

The question hung heavy in the air, a stark reminder of the consequences of his insatiable greed. The carefully constructed facade of a self-made billionaire was collapsing, revealing a man who'd sold his soul for a taste of power.

The next morning, the President braced himself for another onslaught from the media. He entered the press room, the weight of scrutiny heavy on his shoulders. The reporters, sensing his vulnerability, swarmed him like piranhas.

"Mr. President," a young, aggressive reporter started, "how do you respond to the accusations of financial misconduct?"

The President squared his shoulders, attempting to project an air of defiance. "I deny any wrongdoing," he stated, his voice strained. "These allegations are politically motivated and without merit."

A chorus of disbelieving murmurs rose from the room. This tired defense, once effective, now rang hollow.

A veteran reporter, a man with a reputation for tough questions, stepped forward. "The evidence suggests otherwise, Mr. President," he said, his voice a low growl. "Over 170 suspicious activity reports. That doesn't sound like a politically motivated witch hunt. That sounds like a mountain of evidence."

The President stared at the reporter, a cornered animal trapped in the media spotlight. "I have nothing to hide," he finally said, the words devoid of conviction. "I will fully cooperate with any investigation."

But the damage was done. The President's carefully constructed world was crumbling around him. The walls were closing in, and the evidence was stacking up like an insurmountable wall. His dream of leaving a legacy of greatness had morphed into a waking nightmare.

The once-untouchable President, now faced the prospect of impeachment, a stain that would forever tarnish his name. The fight for his political survival had begun, but the outcome was far from certain. The storm had arrived, and the President, stripped of his power and his lies, stood exposed in its relentless glare.

The shockwaves from the raids reverberated across the nation like a sonic boom. Images of confiscated wealth – mountains of cash stacked under harsh lights, dazzling jewels glinting on velvet trays, and gold bars that gleamed like miniature suns – splashed across news outlets and social media. These weren't isolated incidents of greed; they were the gruesome trophies of a systemic corruption that had festered for years.

The evidence spoke for itself. The meticulous financial records, the coded messages exchanged with shadowy figures, and the incriminating documents found hidden behind bookcases – it all painted a damning picture. Senator Robbins, once a golden boy of politics, now stood exposed as a kingpin of deceit. President the man who swore to uphold the highest office, appeared to be the architect of a web of lies and dirty money.

The public fury was a tsunami, engulfing the nation's capital. Protests erupted outside the White House, chants of "Lock him up!" echoing through the streets. The President; cornered and sweating, addressed the nation in a televised speech. His face, etched with a poorly disguised desperation, lacked the usual charisma. He denied the allegations, his voice devoid of conviction. It was a performance no one believed, further fueling the flames of public outrage.

The House of Representatives, their hand forced by the sheer weight of evidence, launched a formal impeachment inquiry. The investigation room crackled with tension as Dr. Evans, his jaw set in grim determination, laid out the case before a panel of stern-faced representatives. He presented a timeline of events, meticulously weaving together financial transactions, witness testimonies, and intercepted communications. Each piece fit into a disturbing puzzle, revealing a network of corruption that stretched from the opulent halls of the Senate to the Oval Office itself.

Across the table, the President's defense team, led by the sharp-tongued attorney Ms. Thorne, launched a counteroffensive. Her strategy was audacious – to discredit the entire investigation as a politically motivated witch hunt. She pointed at inconsistencies in witness statements, questioned the validity of financial records, and cast aspersions on the motives of Dr. Evans and his team.

"Dr. Evans," Ms. Thorne said, her voice dripping with contempt, "you seem awfully eager to see the President brought down. Isn't there a possibility your investigation is fueled by personal animus rather than facts?"

Evans met her gaze unflinchingly. "There's nothing personal about this, Ms. Thorne. We simply follow the evidence, wherever it may lead."

The inquiry stretched on for weeks, televised live for the nation to witness. Every witness, every piece of evidence, was dissected with surgical precision. The public became a jury, glued to their screens, their verdict slowly solidifying with each new revelation.

Meanwhile, the walls around President Nate were closing in. Allies started distancing themselves, advisors resigned, and whispers of a potential resignation grew louder. The once-untouchable leader now resembled a caged animal, his desperate attempts to control the narrative met with scorn and ridicule.

One afternoon, during a particularly heated exchange between Ms. Thorne and Congressman Morrison, a bombshell dropped. A whistleblower; a high-ranking official within the President's administration, emerged with a damning recording – an audio tape capturing the President himself negotiating a shady deal with a foreign businessman. The recording was crystal clear, the President's voice unmistakable.

The room erupted in pandemonium. Ms. Thorne's carefully constructed defense crumbled like a house of cards. Congressman Morrison slammed his fist on the table, a triumphant glint in his eyes. "There you have it, ladies and gentlemen! The President, caught red-handed!"

The impeachment inquiry had reached a tipping point. The evidence against President Nate was overwhelming and undeniable. The question now wasn't if he would be impeached, but when. The walls had crumbled, exposing the rotten core of a corrupt administration. The fight for justice had taken a dramatic turn, and the nation held its breath, anticipating the final verdict.

The House hearing room crackled with anticipation. All eyes were on Paul David, the President's nephew, a man whose once carefree demeanor had been replaced by a haunted look. He gripped the armrests of the witness chair, his knuckles white.

"Mr. David," Congressman Seth began, his voice a measured gavel, "you claim the President was aware of the illegal activities within POTUS, his charity foundation."

Paul's voice was a mere rasp. "Not just aware, Congressman. He orchestrated them."

A collective gasp rippled through the room. Seth leaned forward, his gaze sharp. "Strong accusation. Care to elaborate?"

Paul took a deep breath, his eyes darting towards the gallery where a phalanx of cameras captured his every move. "Uncle Newman... the President... always had a soft spot for deals on the fringes of legality. But this... this was different. This was blatant corruption."

He described a web of shell companies, inflated invoices, and "donations" that funneled directly into the President's personal accounts. Names of foreign dignitaries were dropped like ticking time bombs, each one a link in the President's chain of deceit.

"He used POTUS as a slush fund," Paul finished, his voice shaking with a mix of anger and betrayal. "A piggy bank for his own greed."

Across the table, Marcus Stein, the President's former financial advisor, sat like a man facing a firing squad. His tailored suit hung loosely on his once portly frame, his face pale under the harsh fluorescent lights.

"Mr. Stein," Seth said, his voice switching to a conversational tone, "you were the President's closest confidante financially. Corroborate Mr. David's claims?"

Stein, his gaze flickering nervously between Seth and the President's stoic face in the gallery, swallowed hard. "The evidence... Mr. David's account... it aligns with what I witnessed."

His voice, barely a whisper, echoed in the room. The damning admission hung in the air, a death knell for the President's carefully constructed facade.

The following days were a blur of testimonies. Witnesses, both high-ranking officials and low-level employees, painted a picture of a President systematically enriching himself, under the guise of philanthropy. Each testimony chipped away at the President's remaining support in the House.

In the heavily guarded confines of the Oval Office, the President watched his world crumble through the filter of a television screen. His once vibrant face was now a mask of impotent rage.

"This is a witch hunt!" he bellowed, slamming his fist on the Resolute Desk. "They're twisting everything!"

His Chief of Staff, a man named Harris, watched him with a weary resignation. "Mr. President, the evidence..."

"Don't tell me about evidence!" the President roared, cutting him off. "There's no evidence! It's all lies!"

But even Harris could see the truth reflected in the President's bloodshot eyes. The carefully crafted narrative of a benevolent leader had been replaced by the stark reality of a corrupt politician cornered and desperate.

"Mr. President," Harris said, his voice low, "we may need to consider your options."

The President's face contorted in a mix of defiance and fear. "Options? What options? I'm not going down without a fight!"

Harris sighed. Denial was no longer a strategy. The House Judiciary Committee, after weeks of grueling deliberations, released their findings. It was a damning indictment; a comprehensive document detailing the President's financial misconduct, abuse of power, and blatant disregard for the law.

"The evidence presented today is irrefutable," boomed the Committee Chairman, his voice amplified across the nation via television. "The President has engaged in a pattern of criminal behavior that cannot be ignored."

Representative Johnson stepped forward, his face thunderous. "These violations of the law and abuse of power cannot be tolerated. We must act decisively to protect the integrity of our democracy."

The room erupted in a cacophony of shouts and murmurs. The die was cast. The House was prepared to vote on impeachment. With the weight of public opinion and a mountain of evidence against him, the President's dreams of a second term lay shattered. The walls had closed in, and the man who once reveled in power now faced the prospect of a humiliating downfall.

The air in the White House Situation Room hung heavy with a suffocating mix of desperation and stale coffee. President Nate, his once-booming voice reduced to a raspy croak, slumped at the head of the table. His advisors, a group of usually impeccably tailored sharks, now resembled cornered rats, their eyes darting nervously around the room.

"Gentlemen," President Nate began, his voice cracking under the weight of the moment. "We all know, why we're here."

No one dared to meet his gaze. The elephant in the room was as large and as unwelcome as a nuclear warhead. Impeachment. The word hung in the air, an unspoken death knell for Nate's presidency.

"The damn committee..." John Harris, the President's Chief of Staff, finally broke the silence. His voice was laced with a bitterness that mirrored the mood in the room. "Their report is a goddamn lynch mob with a briefcase."

"There's still a chance," interjected Ella Maxfield, the President's steely press secretary. Her voice, usually a weapon of mass deflection, lacked its usual conviction.

"A chance of what, Lily?" Nate snapped, a flicker of his old fire momentarily rekindled in his eyes. "Of them spontaneously forgetting all the evidence against me? Of Paul and Stein suddenly changing their tunes?"

The room fell silent again. Paul, the President's own nephew, and Stein, his trusted financial advisor, had turned into Judas goats, their testimonies damning indictments of the President's involvement in the POTUS scandal.

"There has to be something that we can do," David Clarke, the President's legal counsel, finally mumbled, more to himself than anyone else.

"We discredit the witnesses," Thompson said, her voice hardening. "Dig up dirt, inconsistencies, anything to cast doubt on their motives."

A flicker of hope flickered in Nate's eyes. "Yes! Dig, smear, whatever it takes! Make them look like liars, like pawns in someone else's game."

But even as the President spoke, a chilling realization dawned on Harris. It was a desperate gamble, a last-ditch effort to cling to a sinking ship. Public opinion had turned against Nate, and the evidence against him was irrefutable.

"Mr. President," Harris finally dared to say, his voice laced with a quiet resignation, "the odds... they're not in our favor."

Nate slammed his fist on the table, the sound echoing through the tense room. "Don't you dare talk to me about odds, Harris! I built this empire on long shots and Hail Mary's. We'll fight this, tooth and nail!"

But even Nate's bluster couldn't mask the growing fear in his eyes. He knew, deep down, that the game was over. The walls were closing in, and the once-untouchable President was about to face the ultimate political judgment. The fight for his legacy had become a desperate scramble for survival, and the outcome was far from certain.

Chapter Twenty
Epilogue: A Tale Of Corruption And Justice

Inside the hallowed halls of the House of Representatives, tension hung in the air like a suffocating fog. Whispers of conspiracy and betrayal echoed through the chambers as lawmakers prepared for a momentous vote - a vote that could shake the foundations of the nation.

Outside the White House, a seething crowd had gathered, their voices rising in a crescendo of anger and discontent. Signs held high, they chanted with fervor, demanding justice.

"We want him out!"

"He's a disgrace to our country!"

"No more corruption!"

Within the Senate, the stage was set for a historic showdown. The fate of the presidency rested on the shoulders of these solemn jurors, tasked with the weighty responsibility of trying the case. The evidence against the President was damning, and the stakes couldn't be higher.

As the House voted to impeach him, the final blow was dealt. The Speaker of the House declared, "The House of Representatives has voted to impeach the President of the United States." The news reverberated through the nation, shattering the once impenetrable fortress of the White House. The President's grip on power was slipping, and the realization of his downfall cast a pall over the corridors of power.

The trial that followed was a spectacle unlike any other, captivating the attention of millions around the globe. The nation watched with bated breath as the evidence against the President was laid bare, each revelation more damning than the last. The courtroom buzzed with a mix of anticipation and trepidation, the air heavy with the weight of the truth.

Morrison, Robbins, and even the President's own nephew, Paul, took the stand. Their voices trembled with conviction and regret as they recounted their experiences, exposing the President's web of deceit and corruption. Whispers of secret deals, backroom meetings, and financial misconduct swirled through the courtroom, each revelation tightening the noose around the President's neck.

With each passing day of the trial, the President's once defiant demeanor crumbled. His confident facade shattered, revealing a man on the brink of collapse. He knew the overwhelming evidence against him was indisputable, and the walls of his once impenetrable fortress began to close in.

In backrooms and private conversations, powerful figures whispered their concerns, weighing their options. The President's allies grappled with their loyalty, torn between their allegiance and the undeniable truth. The tension between them simmered, threatening to boil over into a dangerous confrontation.

As the trial neared its climax, the courtroom crackled with electricity. The President's fate hung in the balance, teetering on the precipice of justice. The prosecutors and defense attorneys clashed, their arguments propelled by a desperate determination to sway the jury.

The tension in the Senate chamber crackled like electricity. All eyes were glued to the giant screen displaying the final vote count. 60... 61... 62... The gavel slammed down, silencing the hushed whispers. "Guilty!" the voice boomed.

President Nate; a pale imitation of his former self, slumped in his chair, his face a mask of disbelief. The verdict echoed through the chamber, a death knell for his once-unshakeable reign.

Across the nation, a collective sigh of relief swept through living rooms and bars alike. People erupted in cheers, the sound a tidal wave washing away months of anxiety and anger. Justice, though delayed, had finally prevailed.

The news reached the White House Situation Room like a thunderclap. Advisors, already packing their belongings, exchanged grim glances. John Harris, the Chief of Staff, met Ella Wayne's gaze, a shared sense of finality hanging between them. The fight was over.

"Mr. President," Harris said, his voice devoid of its usual bravado, "the car is waiting."

Nate, his eyes vacant, stared at the resolute seal on the carpet. The weight of his crimes, the crumbling facade of power, finally crushed him. He rose, a broken man, and shuffled towards the exit, his once-proud steps heavy with defeat.

The following days were a whirlwind of activity. Nate, his spirit broken, offered a half-hearted resignation speech, his pleas for forgiveness falling on deaf ears. The nation watched with a mix of sadness and disgust as the first President ever to be convicted was escorted out of the White House; a cautionary tale etched in history.

As the dust settled, the task force, led by the stoic Speaker of the House, allowed themselves a moment of quiet satisfaction. They had navigated a political minefield, weathered relentless attacks, and exposed a web of corruption that reached the very top. The road had been long and fraught with danger, but they had emerged victorious.

"We did it," the Speaker said, addressing the task force. "We held a President accountable."

A tired smile played on Dr. Evans' lips, the lead investigator who had spearheaded the case. "We did," he said, his voice hoarse from countless hours spent digging through evidence. "But the fight for justice is never truly over."

The nation, though divided, began the slow process of healing. The scars of the scandal ran deep, but there was a renewed sense of hope. The delicate balance of power had been restored, a stark reminder that no one, no matter how powerful, stood above the law. The fight against corruption, however, was far from over. The task force, their job complete, disbanded, leaving behind a legacy of resilience and a clear message: in the face of overwhelming evidence, even the most powerful walls crumble, and justice, however delayed, will ultimately prevail.

Years later, the echoes of Operation Blind Allegiance still resonated through the halls of power. The scandal had become a cautionary tale, a twisted morality play etched into the nation's collective memory. President Nate's face, once a symbol of unwavering authority, now served as a mugshot in history books, a stark reminder of the perils of unchecked ambition.

The impact of the operation stretched far beyond the Oval Office. Whistleblower hotlines buzzed with newfound activity, citizens emboldened by the knowledge that even the most powerful could be brought down. Investigative journalists, once treated with suspicion, were now hailed as heroes, their relentless pursuit of truth a vital check on the system.

But the ghosts of Operation Blind Allegiance lingered. Ella Maxfield, the President's former press secretary, became a recluse, haunted by her complicity. John Harris, the Chief of Staff, disappeared from the public eye, his reputation forever tarnished. As for President Nate, a shell of his former self, he retreated to a secluded estate, the weight of his conviction a crushing burden.

One quiet evening, Dr. Evans, the lead investigator, sat in his dimly lit study, a worn copy of the Senate's impeachment report resting on his desk. He flipped through the pages; memories of the grueling investigation flooding back. The sleepless nights, the death threats, the relentless pressure – it all seemed a lifetime ago.

A knock on the door startled him. He opened it to find a young woman, her eyes filled with a determined glint. "Dr. Evans?" she asked, her voice steady. "My name is Cara Turner. I have some information..."

Evans ushered her in, a flicker of curiosity igniting in his eyes. The fight for justice, he realized with a weary smile, was a never-ending battle. Operation Blind Allegiance may be over, but the fight against corruption, fueled by the courage of whistleblowers and the tenacity of investigators, will continue.

The walls of power could be breached, and the darkness, however pervasive, could always be challenged by a single spark of truth.